AF485955

THE MACLEOD PIRATE

CAROLINE KORPAN LEE

ABOUT THIS BOOK

The Black Banner is the Western Isles' most notorious pirate... and he's about to meet his match!

Citrine is the last Sinclair Jewel left with any chance to save her clan, and she's not about to fail them. But when she's a victim of mistaken identity and taken prisoner by a gorgeous —and completely maddening—pirate captain, Citrine is afraid she's missed her opportunity. She discovers the Black Banner holds one of her family's long-lost jewels, and he refuses to tell her why. Could their pasts--and futures--be somehow connected?

Rory MacLeod is the youngest son of a powerful laird and is happy to let others rule as he spends his life at sea...as the Scourge of the Minch, the fierce pirate known as the Black Banner. When his father signs a betrothal contract with the Sinclair laird, Rory has no intention of following through with it. Little does he realize the beautiful firebrand he's just kidnapped is the woman he's supposed to marry!

Together, Citrine and the Black Banner might be able to solve one mystery…but the real threat to the future of the Sinclairs is back at home.

A lifetime of secrets, a hidden identity, and a bitter hatred will all come to light in this final piece of the gripping Sinclair Jewels saga!

Warning: <u>Scorching hot</u> Highlander romance!

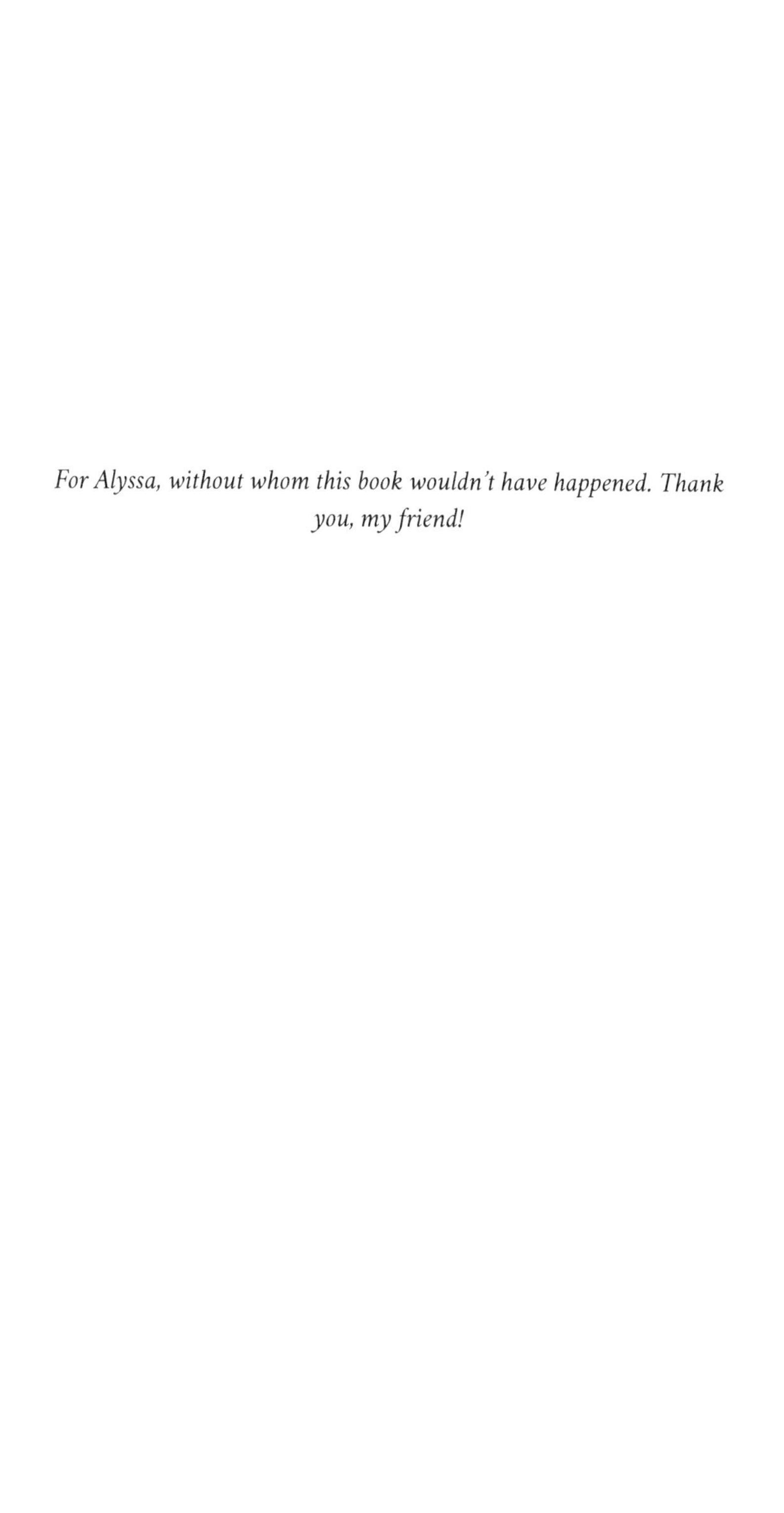

For Alyssa, without whom this book wouldn't have happened. Thank you, my friend!

CHAPTER 1

THE BLADE CHANGED DIRECTIONS MIDAIR, slicing toward her head. Citrine managed to get her short sword up in time to deflect the blow, but the jarring force of the strike left her arms weak.

She spun to the side, flicking her opponent's blade off hers and buying herself a moment's respite to wipe her arm across her brow. The sweat caused her unruly, blonde hair to stick to her forehead, and not for the first time, she lamented the convention which forced her to keep it long.

"Again!" she panted, lifting her sword in the ready position.

William, one of the younger Sinclair warriors, shrugged. "Ye sure, Citrine?"

"Aye! *Again!*"

In response to the command in her tone, William threw himself forward, his blade flashing in the summer afternoon sunlight. She parried one, then two strikes, before he made use of the earlier technique.

She stopped him easier this time. Knowing she couldn't hold him for long—his arms were stronger than hers, after all —she held up a hand. "Hold."

William immediately stepped back, a smirk on that face she'd once thought handsome. "Had enough?"

Enough? Aye, she was worn down…but not beaten.

Never beaten.

She'd been a young girl when she'd first snuck out to watch her father's men train, and no one had stopped her. That progressed to training on her own, to now, where she trained *with* the men. Her father's commander, Dougal, disapproved, but Da hadn't objected, so the men allowed it.

Still, it was days like today that she wondered why she pushed herself.

Ye could always go practice yer embroidery.

The thought made her snort, a wry grin creeping across her face.

"Show me," she commanded.

The young man's smirk changed to a frown. "What?"

She stifled her sigh. To think she'd once had *feelings* for him! Could she even call William a man? He wasn't much older than her, but he'd proven his worth as a warrior earlier this summer, when he'd been one of the only survivors of an attack on her younger sister, Pearl.

Still, she eyed him derisively. His thin shoulders and slight frame might once have inspired desire in her, but no longer.

The fact he insisted on hiding the wounds he received during that bandit attack by wearing a tunic even during training…well, suffice it to say she was no longer impressed.

"*Show me,*" she repeated louder. Settling into position, she gestured him to attack. "Slower this time, so I might learn. 'Tis why I'm here, after all."

From the frown on his face, it was clear he didn't think she should be there at all. "And 'tis my responsibility to teach ye?"

She huffed and rolled her eyes, lifting her sword higher. "Come now, William. Ye perfect yer own skills by teaching, ye ken that."

When he still looked unconvinced and glanced toward another pair of sparring partners, she tried another tactic. Clearing her throat, she forced a contrite expression. "Please?"

The *please* must've done it, because he sighed and took up position. "*Fine.* I suppose I can do a pretty lass a favor or two."

She might've objected to his meaning if he hadn't *finally* consented to attack her again, and her focus was taken up by studying his moves. After the third round, she was ready to try the move on *him,* and was pleased to see her attack was quick enough to cause him to fumble to raise his hand and block her.

And so they went, back and forth, studying one another for weaknesses to exploit and throwing taunts.

The taunting was a typical part of training among the Sinclair warriors, but most avoided it with Citrine. Only William bothered, and only because of what they'd once shared.

When she'd been younger, she had fancied herself in love with the lad. And whether or not it had been honorable, he'd taken what had been offered. She'd lost her virginity in the stables in a thoroughly unsatisfying encounter. The second and third times had been pleasant enough, but when she'd realized he wasn't at all interested in her pleasure, she'd told him never again.

And mayhap he hadn't forgiven her for that, judging from the bitterness in his eyes as he waited for her to attack once more.

"Have ye learned it, lass?"

She blew out a breath and lifted an eyebrow, refusing to show how exhausted she was. "Ye tell me!"

Her blows landed swift and hard, and she heard him grunt as he stumbled back. The realization she had unbalanced him brought a grim smile to her lips, but she didn't let up on her attack. It wasn't until he cursed and spun out of the way that she let up, but that was a mistake. He only dropped, swiping at her knees.

She almost didn't see the new tactic, although she should've. Exhaustion had stolen her attention and speed, but when she realized the blade was prepared to take out her legs, she leapt…and landed wrong, her left leg buckling.

With a grunt, she went down, rolling, and forcing herself up to her knees.

This was training, aye, but she'd always demanded the men not go easy on her. She wanted to learn, to be valuable to the clan, and she couldn't do that by giving up and staying on the ground when she fell.

Get up.

Another grunt as she shoved one leg under her, only to see William lift his sword in a begrudging salute.

Confused, she lifted her own, albeit slower, and frowned when he moved away. By all the saints, was he conceding? Because she hadn't conceded his win, and what would cause him—

Oh.

Standing to one side of the training area with his arms crossed in front of his still-powerful chest, Laird Duncan Sinclair was frowning at her.

Doing her best to hide her exhaustion, she forced herself to her feet, pulled a rag from her belt, and made a show of wiping down her blade before lovingly sliding it back into the scabbard at her hip.

She used the same rag to wipe her forehead and neck, tucking the stray hairs behind her ears and thinking longingly of the loch's cool water. Then, and only then, did she move toward her father.

"Hello, Da," she called cheerfully as she got closer. "Here to watch me kick William's arse?"

Mayhap it was the right greeting. Almost reluctantly, his

scowl eased. "Ye *were* doing quite well. The lad isnae the right partner for ye, though."

Her brows rose as she settled her fists on her hips. As every day, she wore a tunic belted loosely over a pair of trews. Her feet were bare, but her boots lay in the grass up on the hill where she and her sisters used to sit to watch the men train.

"Ye think I need a better partner?" What did Da know of her history with William?

"The lad isnae a bad opponent, but he doesnae challenge ye, Citrine. Ye need a challenge."

She leapt at the opportunity. "So ye're saying I should train with Dougal and the aulder warriors?" It was a right denied to the youngest among them…and most definitely to the laird's *daughter*.

"Nay, lass." He shook his head almost regretfully. "I'm saying ye need a different kind of challenge. The sword doesnae challenge ye anymore."

With a sinking feeling, Citrine took the waterskin he offered her. "What would?" she asked dully, suspecting she knew the answer.

"Being a wife and mother. Walk with me."

He didn't wait to see if she objected but turned toward the keep. Citrine followed, the waterskin dangling from one hand as she focused on the path ahead of her.

Wife and mother, bah!

At the start of the new year, Da had suddenly begun talking about marriage contracts for his four daughters. Mother had been long gone, and without sons to follow him, Da was obviously concerned with ensuring his daughters' safety.

Pearl—the youngest of Citrine's sisters—had been betrothed to the Sutherland laird, but had broken that contract to marry Da's longtime bodyguard, the Sinclair Hound. Their oldest sister was now happily married to the Mackenzie regent, and raising the next laird of that clan. And

Citrine's twin sister, Saffy, had only just returned to her new home among the Sutherlands, after having joyfully wed Pearl's old suitor.

She was thrilled for her sisters, for certes. They'd all found love where they didn't expect it, and were settled into their new lives as wives and—aye—even mothers.

But not Citrine.

Her place was here by her father's side, ensuring his rule lasted for as long as possible and keeping her clan together.

But a month ago he'd announced her betrothal to the youngest son of one of the MacLeod clans among the Western Isles. Likely a pock-faced lad, too young to piss off a curtain wall, who cared only for the power an alliance with the once-powerful Sinclairs would bring.

"Da, I dinnae want those things," she began, only to have him raise a hand to cut her off.

"Aye, I ken it, Citrine."

With a sigh, he sank down on one of the boulders lining the path, and she realized he'd led her this way to give them a little privacy for their talk. She was normally too full of energy to sit still, but today…

She sat at his feet, her back to the same boulder, and pulled her knees up to wrap her arms around them.

"Citrine, yer mother and I…we wanted ye to be safe." When she started to object, he continued. "And ye're no' safe here, unmarried. Ye ken I'm getting aulder. The last few months have taught us both that."

Halfway through the summer, Da was laid low by an unexplained stomach ailment. He had grown weaker and weaker, and Citrine had been genuinely afraid she'd lose him.

It wasn't until she began to check his food and ensuring he only ate what she fed him, that he began to improve. It was enough to go to him with her suspicions.

"The last few months have taught us who to trust," she grumbled.

"I ken ye believe I was being poisoned, and I dinnae deny 'tis a possibility. But I also reject yer theory of my enemy. Dougal is no' only my cousin, but has been my second-in-command for many years."

Throwing up her hands, she blew out an exasperated breath. "And the only one who stands to gain, Da!"

She twisted, staring up at him. "Ye *were* being poisoned, and Dougal—"

"Who do ye think will take over the clan when I'm gone, Citrine?" her father quietly interrupted.

Her mouth snapped shut, unwilling to contemplate such a future.

The Sinclair laird let out a tired sounding breath and scrubbed a hand over his thick beard. "I'm no' ready to die yet, daughter, but ye ken I've long considered the possibilities. Without a son to follow me as laird, what other choices do I have? I have nae living brothers, and without the Jewels…"

It took a moment for Citrine to realize he wasn't speaking of her and her sisters. Long called the Sinclair Jewels by the fanciful Highland folk, the four of them had been named for the jewels in the long-missing Sinclair brooch.

That was what her father referred to. Legend had it that the clan's fortune was tied to the jewels, and when it went missing generations ago, the Sinclairs began to lose power. Now, with no sons to take over the clan after him, Duncan Sinclair was obviously convinced his family would fall into obscurity.

But not all hope was lost.

Unbeknown to him, Citrine and her sisters had embarked on a quest to restore not just the jewels, but the clan to honor. After receiving an ancient tapestry from their elderly nurse, Elspeth, the sisters followed a clue to the Mackenzie keep. Agata's journey there—and her adventure to find love with her new husband, Jaimie—resulted in finding the first missing stone, an agate as big as a man's thumb.

The clue they'd found with the stone led the sisters to the Sutherlands, where scholarly Saffy took it upon herself to don a disguise and become a squire to the most-feared man in the Highlands. Their adventures led to love, as well as finding the missing sapphire under a block in the dungeon carved with the clan crest of the MacLeods of Lewes.

The MacLeods of Lewes…the same clan her father would have her marry into.

But she'd resisted leaving him. Lewes was on the other side of Scotland, and how could she keep Da safe—from threats like Dougal—if she went there?

But if one of the two missing stones—a citrine and pearl—was on Lewes, how could she not?

Mayhap it was time to tell Da about the stones she and her sisters had already collected? Mayhap the knowledge that two of the four missing jewels were tucked in a wooden box under her bed would improve his mood?

Mayhap he wouldn't insist she marry then, but would allow her to merely *visit* Lewes to retrieve whatever stone was there?

"I can hear ye thinking over there, wee one." Da's voice was quiet, almost sorrowful. "I ken ye're trying to come up with a way out of this, but ye cannae. My mind is made up."

Citrine uncorked the waterskin. "About what?" she asked dully, knowing she wouldn't like the answer.

He waited for her to take a drink.

"Ye're going to be married, Citrine. Rory MacLeod is a good lad—strong and brave. His father and I agree he'll be a good match for ye. A *challenge*."

"And my wants dinnae matter?"

He chuckled. "Yer sisters have thought to run me in circles, Citrine, choosing their own happiness over the clan's."

She frowned. "All of them married good men, making strong alliances. They didnae need ye to force them to marry."

"Aye, they're good lassies, and now I ken they'll be protected when I'm gone."

That was enough. Despite the wobble in her legs from the sparring, Citrine pushed herself up to loom over her father. "Ye're *no'* going anywhere, Da. I'll make sure."

"Lass…" Shaking his head, her father stood, matching her irritation. "I love ye well, but ye're no' more stubborn than I am. Dougal will no' harm me, and I plan to rule here for a while yet."

She stood on her toes until her nose was inches from his. "But I'll no' be here to see it, that's yer plan? I'll be stuck in some castle that stinks of fish, far from here?"

His lips twitch. "We Sinclairs have a proud seafaring and fishing tradition, lass."

Blowing out a frustrated breath, she sank back to her heels. "Ye ken what I mean, Da." Suddenly tired, she felt the fight drain from her. "Ye really are going to do this?" She peeked up at him.

"Dinnae play meek with me, lass. Ye've kenned about this plan for a while. I only postponed it until I was well and could ensure ye *would* leave. Now I ken what to look for—and aye, I swear, I'll watch for poison. I can do that without ye—ye *will* fulfill the terms of the contract."

Thinking about the marriage contract—signed by Da and the MacLeod—she frowned.

"Och, Citrine."

Da clucked his tongue and, after glancing left and right to ensure they were still alone, pulled her into a hug. She didn't *want* to be comforted—she wanted to maintain her anger, to slowly stoke the flames until they burned bright—but feeling her father's arms around her was too much. She hugged him back, burrowing her face in his shoulder.

"Ye're a good daughter. I raised ye to understand honor and sacrifice, like any good warrior. I ken ye'll do what's right for the Sinclair clan."

Blessed Virgin, why did he have to make it sound so *final*?

Setting her back, he placed his hands on her shoulders and nodded firmly. "Think of it this way, lass: 'Twill be a challenge. One ye've never met afore. If yer marriage is aught like mine with yer mother, 'twill be the greatest adventure ye ever have."

Greatest adventure? She stopped herself from snorting in derision. *Unlikely.* Marriage to a man who would expect her to wear dresses and embroider and do whatever the hell it was *ladies* did all day...?

It did not sound like an adventure, but... "A challenge," she mumbled, staring at Da's beard.

"Aye, a challenge. Ye'll do fine, Citrine."

Slowly, she shifted her gaze to the distant mountain, knowing if she met his eyes, he'd see the beginnings of her plan there.

A challenge, eh?

Aye, she *would* go to the MacLeod holding on Lewes. She *would* meet this pock-faced lad her father had betrothed her to.

She *would* find the missing jewel the MacLeods had been hiding all these years.

And then she'd come back home.

Alone.

Because her place was here, at her father's side. For the future of the Sinclairs.

CHAPTER 2

"One of brown, and one of white,
And one of the deepest blue!
One glows gold in the fire's light,
Jewels in the hearthstone's view!"

The little girl's sweet voice rang pure in the old nursery song as she lined her wooden ships up along the edge of the cold hearth. Rory MacLeod, sprawled in one of the wooden chairs, felt his lips tug upward at the sound.

Wee Charlotte hadn't inherited her mother's flawless voice, but it was her enthusiasm which made him smile. That, and the fact that she was recreating the Battle of Largs with the miniature boats Rory himself used to play with.

"Uncle Rory, what jewels do ye think the song means?"

Shifting slightly, he threw one leg over the chair's arm and hummed thoughtfully. His ever-present, not-quite-good-luck-charm passed from palm to palm as he considered the answer. The dull gleam of the large, oval pearl was comforting, as always.

Finally, he shrugged. "What do *ye* think it means, wee one?"

Charlotte lifted her chin, her red curls falling around her

shoulders as she frowned at him. "I think 'tis *gold*. That's what the song sings about, aye?"

It was her twin brother who objected. Scoffing, Tavish stabbed at imaginary foes in the long afternoon shadows. "The jewels are all different colors, clot-heid. *That's* what the song is about!"

As Char prepared to throw one of the wooden toys at her brother's back, Rory held up his hand for peace. "The song is likely a metaphor, lass. Saying that all the jewels and treasures and gold yer heart needs can be found with yer family."

When his niece rolled her eyes, Rory managed not to snort, but just barely.

"Well, *I* ken that's no' true, Uncle!" Tav leapt effortlessly up to one of the benches, slashing with his wooden blade. "The *real* treasure is the goods ye take yerself! The Black Banner kens where all the treasure is!"

His sister scoffed, her attention once more on the ships preparing to battle. "An' what would a pirate do with wool and grain? Or whatever the merchants are shipping?"

"*Sell it*, obviously!" Tav posed with his sword in the air and one bare foot up on the table, then lowered his voice. "He keeps the wool to dye black for his own menacing sail, and he sells the rest for his own profit!"

This time, Rory did smile. "Menacing, huh?"

"I learned a new word!"

His sister snorted. "Mother says ye should devote yerself to yer studies as hard as to yer training."

"Why?" Tav shrugged. "I'll no' need *reading* or Latin when I'm the Black Banner!"

Char scrambled to her feet. "Ye cannae be the Black Banner! He already exists!"

When Rory dropped his booted feet to the ground, both siblings startled. "The Black Banner is a name, handed down from pirate to pirate for generations. Yer grandda kenned the Black Banner, and he wasnae even the original one."

With wide eyes, Tav slid to the ground. "Is he a MacLeod?"

Rory winked, rolling the pearl between his palms. "The MacLeods have always been a seafaring people, lad. What do ye think?"

Char sidled over to press herself against his leg. "Do *ye* ken him, Uncle Rory?"

"If I told ye, aye, yer brother wouldnae stop pestering me, demanding an introduction."

"Nay!" Tav cried, jamming his wooden sword into the belt holding up his wee tartan. "I mean, I wouldnae. Do ye? Do ye ken him?"

Charlotte tugged at Rory's arm. "*I* wouldnae pester ye either, Uncle Rory, although I want to meet the Black Banner."

"Why, poppet?" Rory tweaked his niece's nose. "So ye can run away and become a pirate as well?"

"Nay," she said seriously. "Tav's going to be the Black Banner. I'm going to be somebody even greater."

Leaning against Rory's other leg, her brother scoffed. "Ye're a *lass*. Ye're going to grow up and get married and have bairns. *That's* no' greatness."

Charlotte stuck her tongue out. "I dinnae have to do that. I'll make our clan proud."

"By getting *married*?"

"Enough!" Rory held his hands up between them. When he had their attention, he began to roll the pearl back and forth between his fingers. "Charlotte, ye can be as great as yer brother, I believe that. And Tav, there's naught wrong with marrying for the benefit of the clan."

"'Tis glad I am to hear it, little brother."

The deep voice from the doorway had Rory standing, uncomfortable with the knowledge his oldest brother had heard his words. Tormund was not only already married, but had fathered half a dozen bairns already, and would one day be the MacLeod chief.

Rory was the youngest of four brothers and half as many sisters. His father was fond of telling him the "least useful of the lot."

Knowing what was expected of him, even if it rankled, Rory nodded in respect. "Yer children and I were discussing responsibilities and their future."

Tormund crossed his arms over his chest, glaring at Rory with blue eyes that matched his own. "And ye were defending yerself to my son?"

Glancing down at Tav, who was staring up adoringly, Rory tried not to wince. He knew well what his brother was referring to and knew what it would mean to his future.

"I was explaining to Tavish that one day, if ye make a marriage alliance for Charlotte's hand, she'll be helping the clan."

He met his brother's eyes and wondered if Tormund would continue the taunting he'd been engaged in for the last month.

"Aye, *she* will be."

Of course. Of course, he'd continue the taunting. Rory sighed.

Tormund pointed a finger at Charlotte. "I've already made an alliance for yer sister, and she's but ten summers. One day, ye'll prove as useful as her…and yer uncle."

The mocking laughter which burst from his lips made Rory snarl, but he tamped down the urge to pay his brother back in kind.

One day, Tormund would be his laird, and Rory would live on Lewes at his leisure. Or rather, his *wife* would.

Their other two brothers were both already married and living with their wives. One here on Lewes, and the other on the mainland in holdings their father had granted them. As the youngest and the wanderer of the siblings, Rory had always known he'd have no permanent home on Lewes…but once he was married, his wife would likely require it.

So, he put up with Tormund's mocking, knowing he'd spend the rest of his life returning to this keep to visit his wife as necessary.

By His Wounds, but this situation rankled.

Tormund's laughter ceased as Charlotte pressed against Rory's side, and he dropped his hand to his niece's shoulder. None of his brothers were gentlemen—and neither was he—but it was obvious Tormund's children feared him.

"The two of ye deserve each other," Tormund growled, his eyes narrowing. "Both only useful to the clan through yer *marriage alliances.*"

Tavish frowned, his hand dropping to his wooden blade. Before his father noticed, Rory drew attention with a mocking bow. "'Tis a good thing Father had one unmarried son when the Sinclair came offering one of his Jewels, aye? I live to be *useful* to the clan."

His older brother dropped his fists to his hips. "'Tis the only way ye *can* be, what with ye gallivanting all over the Minch and the Isles, trading. *Trade,*" he spat like it was a curse. "A waste of a warrior's skills."

Dropping his other hand to Tav's shoulder, Rory nodded. "Aye, ye're likely correct, brother. Did ye have need of me for some reason?"

"Aye." Tormund glared at the three of them. "Father is meeting with Tosh's da now about the mess the wee lad made of the kitchens. After he metes out punishment, he wants to see *ye* to discuss yer upcoming nuptials."

Nuptials. The word caused a sour taste to rise in Rory's throat, but he bowed his head in acknowledgment. "I live to serve."

His oldest brother made a noise between a scoff and a curse before stalking out of the room.

The two bairns said nothing as Rory sank back into the chair with his elbows on his knees, gazing sightlessly at the pearl rolling between his fingers once more.

Nuptials. Marriage.

He'd never had an urge to tie himself to one woman, but if he *had*, 'twould be to a woman of his own choosing. Now he kenned how his sisters must've felt when Father announced their marriage contracts.

He spent his life at sea and loved it. It wasn't so much the sailing which held his heart but the *control.* As the youngest of the MacLeods, he'd had so little control over his life growing up. But on the sea, in his birlinn...*he* was in command. *His* decisions dictated success or failure, *his* leadership meant his men lived or died.

And despite Father and Tormund's attempts to take it from him, they'd not succeed.

"What did he mean, Uncle Rory?" Tav's wee voice was accompanied by a frown.

Rory sighed. "Yer grandda has decided to align with the Sinclairs. They're a large clan far to the east of the Highlands with many daughters. Their father offered one of his daughters to our chief, who decided I would marry her."

Charlotte grunted as she poked him in the thigh. "So, 'tis no' just lassies who must marry to form alliances for the clan?"

"Nay, Char." He smiled sadly at her. "The difference is most warriors get a choice who they're to marry. They *choose* to make alliances. 'Tis why yer father taunts me."

The lass folded her arms and frowned fiercely, looking like her da. "When I'm grown, I'm going to be a warrior and *choose* who to marry and align with. Da willnae make me."

Her twin snorted. "Uncle Rory is proof even warriors sometimes dinnae get a choice."

He was right.

"*But!*" Tav pulled his sword from his belt with a flourish.

"When I'm the Black Banner, I'll make sure ye dinnae have to marry an ugly, auld wart-head, Char!"

"Aye!" Charlotte grabbed one of the miniature ships, brandishing it like a weapon. "And I'll make sure nae money-hungry lass gets her hooks into ye either, Captain!"

Rory dropped his chin to his chest so they'd not see his smile. *Get her hooks into ye?* That sounded like something Tormund would say.

"If ye were a pirate, Uncle Rory, ye wouldnae need to do what Grandda says." Tav's savage frown spoke of the warrior he'd one day be. "Ye could run away and join the Black Banner's fleet, and he'd no' force ye to marry."

It was something he'd considered, if he were being honest with himself.

Reaching out, Rory ruffled his favorite nephew's hair. The twins were not the only MacLeod bairns running around the keep. They had older siblings and cousins. But they *were* Rory's favorites, because of their fierce personalities. Whenever he returned to the keep—it was difficult to think of it as *home*—he made sure to search them out and give them little gifts or stories of his adventures.

Mostly embellished, of course.

"If I were a pirate, Tavish, I'd spend most of my days at sea, aye?"

"Aye!" The lad nodded.

"And I'd only return home occasionally, as I do now."

Charlotte poked his thigh again. "Would ye bring yer lady wife with ye on yer adventures?"

"Do ye think she'd enjoy it?"

His niece frowned. "Nay. Most lassies arenae like me, ye ken. At least, 'tis what my nurse is always saying. I think most would prefer to stay in the keep and sew."

Rory nodded solemnly. "Aye, I suspect ye're right. So..." With a sigh, he planted his hands on his thighs and pushed himself upright. "If I'm off adventuring most of my life and my lady wife is here with ye and yer family, perfecting her embroidery…then what does it matter? I'll still be able to lead the life I love."

Tav nodded again. "And now ye'll have three reasons to come back to Lewes! Her, me, and Charlotte."

With a smile, Rory gently brushed the hair from both of their foreheads. "Aye," he said quietly. "But ye'll still be my favorite reason to return here."

"Ye're secret's safe with us, Uncle," Charlotte said solemnly.

"And now…" Rory straightened his shoulders. "I'd better go see what yer grandda wants."

He slipped the pearl into his sporran, but his niece grabbed his hand before he could pull away.

"If ye wanted, I could hold yer pearl for ye, Uncle Rory. I *am* a lady, ye ken, and ladies deserve jewels. 'Tis what Mother tells Father."

Not even bothering to hide his smile, Rory tugged on one of her ears. "Ye're only a lady when it suits ye, eh, lassie?" Before she could reply, he answered her question. "Nay, the pearl isnae yers. I take it with me on all my voyages, ye ken."

Tav bounced on his heels. "'Tis a good-luck charm, then?"

Reluctantly, Rory shook his head. "No'…exactly."

In fact, the pearl had never shown any luck one way or the other, but it had become a part of him that he was reluctant to leave behind. He'd found it many years before in a secret compartment in the headboard of his mother's bed when he'd been playing where he wasn't supposed to. He'd pressed a design—still wasn't sure which one—and a wee door had opened, depositing the stone into his hand.

It was valuable, aye, but more so, it felt important somehow. Not to *him*, but mayhap to his clan. It was the one piece of MacLeod history he'd ever cared about, and he didn't even know what it meant.

But it was *his*, and as the youngest of seven siblings, that was a rare and special thing to say. So, he offered his niece and nephew a smile.

"The pearl is mine. I dinnae ken how I ken it, but I do. One day, it'll lead me to the best treasure of all."

"The treasure waiting at home for ye?" Charlotte breathed reverently.

His wife would one day wait for him here in this keep. Would she be a treasure?

But he couldn't allow Char to doubt. "Aye," he choked. "'Tis likely what it means."

Soon, he'd be tied to this holding by something greater than bonds of birth and brotherhood.

Soon, he'd have a wife here, and eventually bairns to return to.

Soon...but no' yet.

He had a few weeks before this Sinclair daughter was supposed to arrive, and he'd use them well. He'd round up Bull and the lads and they'd take to the seas one last time. Father couldn't object, as long as he swore to return before his betrothed arrived.

His mind set, Rory ruffled the twins' hair once more. "Ye two be good while I'm gone, aye?"

"Aye, Uncle Rory," they chorused, then Tav piped up. "Bring us something good!"

Chuckling, Rory headed for the door. "I will if ye let yer sister win the next time ye swordfight."

"He doesnae need to *let* me!" Charlotte screeched as Tav began to laugh, and Rory stepped into the hall.

He patted the pearl at the pouch on his belt and set off toward his father's solar.

One last adventure. By all the saints, let it be a good one.

CHAPTER 3

"How about this blue dress?"

Citrine hummed distractedly, not looking up from the small box which held all the evidence they'd managed to gather. "Nay, ye keep it."

Her youngest sister, Pearl, who was helping her pack for her journey to the MacLeod holding on Lewes, gave an unladylike snort. "The way Gregor's been feeding me since he discovered I was pregnant, I willnae be able to fit into this dress ere long!"

Smiling, Citrine finally lifted her gaze and raised a brow at her sister. "Ye cannae be so far along as all that. When will my nephew be arriving?"

"Yer *niece* should be here in spring."

"See?" Pointing to prove a point, Citrine smiled. "Ye're no' all *that* pregnant. Take the dress and enjoy it. 'Twill look nice with yer eyes."

With a huff, Pearl dropped the dark blue gown on the pile of other dresses Citrine had already given her. The four sisters had shared this chamber most of their lives, and their gowns as well. When Agata and Saffy went off to be wives, they'd taken some clothes but left much behind. This left more than a dozen gowns for Citrine to use…which she was now ensuring the youngest Sinclair Jewel would have, even if Pearl *was* living in a cottage in the village.

"Ye ken I can see what ye're doing, aye?"

Citrine didn't respond to Pearl's question but turned back to the box, which was open. Carefully, she folded the old tapestry to place inside.

"*Citrine*. I said I ken what ye're doing."

"And what is that?"

Pearl threw herself across the bed, frowning at her sister. "Ye're trying to get rid of all these gowns so the next woman here doesnae get them."

As Citrine's head snapped up and her anger flared, she thought for a moment that Pearl meant Da might marry again. But nay, she was talking about the next laird. He would have a wife, and she'd live in this keep.

"I'm no' letting Dougal become laird after Da," she growled, eyes narrowing at her sister. "He'll no' bring in a woman to steal our things."

Pearl sighed. "And how will ye stop it? No' only is he Da's commander—and *has* been—but he's a cousin. Of sorts." She shrugged. "His grandmother was our great-grandda's second wife, aye?"

"Aye," Citrine snapped, "But that doesnae make him laird."

"Did ye read Saffy's letter?" Pearl asked, obviously trying to change the subject.

It worked. Citrine's eyes went wide. "She wrote? Where is it?"

Frowning, Pearl pointed to a rolled parchment sitting atop one of the trunks Citrine had already packed. "I told ye I put it there. I *kenned* ye werenae paying attention to me!"

Mumbling an excuse, Citrine hurried across the room, damning the skirts she was forced to wear. She snatched up the letter from her twin and sank to the trunk to read it, her eyes skimming the familiar hand.

DEAREST SISTERS,

I cannae believe how happy I am. The return journey was slow, as my husband insisted on pampering me. Since learning of my condition, he has no' allowed me to spar with him once in the court-yard. I ken Citrine will understand the ignominy of that. And I ken Pearl will understand when I say his gentleness doesnae extend to the bedroom, for which I am pleased.

CITRINE ROLLED HER EYES, perfectly aware of her sisters' habits of rutting with their husbands with little provocation. She was no ignorant virgin, but she had no idea how they could possibly allow themselves to lose control so easily.

THE CELEBRATION the Sutherland people gave in honor of our marriage, lasted three full days. I am pleased to report that Gavin and Merrick seem to have healed their friendship, although I wonder if things will go back to the way they were. Poor Elana is recovering from her ordeal, which is a blessing, and the children are a joy.

Citrine, I look forward to one day introducing ye to Maggie; she believes a woman has every right to fight beside her brothers, and with a brother like Becks, she needs all the help she can get! I believe Mary and Adelaide are most like me in their joy of learning, but I look forward to helping the others grow into strong adults.

Adelaide was actually a help to me recently.

Citrine, ye asked me to continue researching the missing jewels, and I believe her idea was a good one. At her suggestion, I wrote to the Campbell clan's historian.

Dear sister, there were four Campbell sisters, all those years ago.

One married our great-grandfather. Two went to the Mackenzie and Sutherland clans, becoming Jaimie and Merrick's grandmothers.

But the fourth sister went to the MacLeods.

That is why we found the sapphire under the MacLeod crest, Citrine—I am sure of it!

I ken Da has betrothed ye to one of the MacLeods, and I ken equally well ye have nae desire to go through with it. Ye likely arenae even planning on staying there, are ye? But this evidence, along with the location of the sapphire 'tis compelling.

If ye willnae marry the MacLeod warrior, will ye go to investigate the missing jewel?

My love to everyone,

Saffy

CITRINE LET the parchment dangle from her fingers as she stared at the worn, wooden floor. A fourth Campbell sister. 'Twas compelling evidence that the MacLeods *did* have something to do with her clans missing jewels.

"Was she right?" Pearl's quiet words jerked Citrine's attention. "About no' planning on staying at Lewes? Are ye even planning on marrying the man Da picked out for ye?"

Citrine swallowed down the burst of guilt. "Ye're one to talk, Pearl. Ye demanded to take *holy vows* afore marrying Da's choice for ye."

"Aye, and am glad I did so." Pearl sat up in the bed, pulling her legs under her. "If I'd married Merrick Sutherland as Da wanted, Saffy wouldnae be so blissfully in love right now… and neither would I. But I'm asking about *ye*."

With a muttered curse, Citrine rolled the parchment once more and threw it on the trunk. "I am betrothed to the man, but 'tis as far as 'twill go. I plan to travel to Lewes to find the missing jewels. And once I discover what I can, I'll return."

"Here."

Frowning at her sister, Citrine stomped back to the table where she'd left the open box. "Aye, *here*. My home. Where I'm needed. Ye're breeding, and ye live with Gregor now. 'Tis up to *me* to protect Da from Dougal."

Pearl blew out a breath. "Ye really think Dougal is a danger? Da obviously doesnae think so."

"Well, Da is blinded by his history with the man, I suppose."

"Da has ruled this clan for longer than either of us have been alive."

Snatching up the pouch containing the large agate their oldest sister had found, Citrine shook it at her sister. "So, what would ye have me do? Ignore my instincts? Ignore the fact my father—my *clan*—might need my help?" With a snarl, she tossed the pouch into the box atop the tapestry. "And travel to the other side of the kingdom to marry a lad who cannae lift a sword with two hands."

Pearl snorted softly. "Ye're being dramatic. Da said yer betrothed is a younger son, 'tis all. *Ye're* a younger daughter. It means naught."

"Aye, but—" Citrine bit down on the confession she'd been about to make and reached for the sapphire they'd wrapped in leather.

But her intuitive sister, used to understanding those around her, guessed.

"But if ye insult him," Pearl said quietly, "'twill be easier to hate him when ye meet him?"

Citrine's fingers tightened around the stone. "I dinnae *want* to marry him, Pearl. I dinnae want to live in some damp and cold castle on an island. I dinnae even like *fish*."

With a small, pitying noise, Pearl stood and crossed to the table. She wrapped her arms around Citrine.

"I ken, sister. I do." Pearl placed a kiss on her cheek. "Ye are the strongest of us all, and if *anyone* can defy tradition and

Da's alliance contracts, 'tis ye. Just try no' to start a war while ye're at it, all right?"

With a snort, Citrine returned the hug, then straightened. "All I want is to find the rest of the jewels, so Da will cease believing the Sinclairs are losing power. We *are* powerful!"

Pearl smiled and stepped back, her hands clasped in front of her. "Well, the legend says only the bravest and cleverest of the Sinclair warriors can return the stones and the clan's glory."

Citrine snorted again, carefully placing the sapphire beside the agate. "And if he could do that, he could become the next laird, eh?"

There was a twinkle in Pearl's voice when she said, "Mayhap," which caused Citrine to glance up. But her sister was only smiling innocently.

When Citrine frowned at her, Pearl turned away, gesturing to the piles of gowns. "I ken ye're intent on returning, but if ye dinnae bring some of these, Da will grow suspicious. I'll pack the trunks. Do ye care which ones I send with ye?"

"Nay," she muttered, distracted. Her sister was right. She *would* have to take enough clothes to make their father think she was moving to Lewes for good. She sighed. "Save yer favorites, I guess, and send the rest with me."

Pearl bustled about, while Citrine did her best to help—or at least, not get in the way. The youngest of the Sinclair Jewels was good at making others feel comfortable, and soon she had Citrine's spirits lifted.

"What will ye do with the stones ye've collected already?" Pearl suddenly asked.

Citrine crossed back to the table, carefully closed the lid to the box, and picked it up. It was only slightly bigger than her hand, and surely no one would expect what power it contained? "I dinnae want to leave it here. I plan to return, aye, but with nae one to protect it..." She shook her head and held it out to her sister. "Ye take it. Keep it safe in yer home."

Pearl was already shaking her head as she stepped back. "Nay, Citrine. Gregor is a fine warrior, aye, but I am no'. And I am rarely home during the day." She spent her hours among the clan, helping and offering guidance in the village. "I couldnae leave it in the cottage if I wasnae there, but if I carried it with me, I could no' protect it."

Frowning, Citrine stared down at the small bundle. Pearl was right; she wasn't the one to protect the jewels. She could ask Gregor, but Citrine wasn't sure how much her silent brother-in-law knew of their mission, and she'd never ask him to keep such a secret from his laird.

With a sigh, she knew it would be best to give the jewels and the tapestry to Da. He could protect them, and mayhap it would improve his outlook.

But if he had the jewels, Dougal would know. Could she risk something happening to them before they were reunited?

"Ye must take them with ye, Citrine," her sister said quietly, closing her hands over the top of the box. "Ye have been the driving force behind this mission, so 'tis up to ye to keep these jewels safe until ye find the last two."

Citrine's lips curved upward at the thought. "Aye," she whispered hoarsely. "*Aye.*" She placed one hand atop Pearl's. "The pearl and the citrine are still missing, ye ken."

Pearl returned her smile. "I ken it. And I trust ye to find them, so that I can pass on the story to my daughter."

"I swear it," Citrine whispered. "I want yer bairns—and Saffy's and Agata's—to ken the power of the Sinclair jewels."

"Oh…" Pearl smiled and pulled her hand from the box to place over her heart. "I suspect they do."

The Sinclair Jewels.

Aye, her nieces and nephews, those by marriage—thinking of Callan and Merrick's brood—and those yet to be born…they would all ken of the Sinclair Jewels, their mothers.

"Go," Pearl said with a wink. "Prove to Da that the Sinclair name is still important and powerful, for all that he only has daughters."

"Aye." With a quick nod, Citrine pushed the box into a leather bag she could sling from her shoulder. "And *ye* swear to me ye'll keep Da safe. Yer Hound is no' to let him eat aught Dougal offers."

Pearl's expression had turned solemn once more. "I dinnae think Gregor believes Dougal is a threat—the man has been Gregor's commander for many years, ye ken. But if I ask for his pledge, I believe he'll understand the urgency."

"Good."

Mayhap Dougal *wasn't* a threat. Mayhap Da's stomach ailment hadn't been poison at all. Or mayhap it *had*, but there was another unseen enemy lurking while Citrine focused on the commander.

Quietly, she cursed under her breath. If there *was* another enemy, this wasn't the time for her to be leaving her father to go gallivanting to the other side of the country.

But she'd be back. She slung the bag over her shoulder, the vow repeating in her heart.

I will return.

She glanced around the room, the chamber she and her sisters had shared for so many years. It had been the lady's chambers, but their long-dead mother had preferred to share Da's bedchamber. There was Saffy's favorite window seat, and the wooden headboard decorated with ornate ivy leaves Agata had painted one winter. There was the brick inside the hearth with the carved eye Pearl had always thought was frightening, and the wooden stool with the embroidered cushion Citrine had tripped over five years before and broken her ankle.

This was her *home*.

I will return.

Pearl pulled her in for another hug. "Good luck, dear sister."

Citrine hugged her back. "I love ye."

———

THEY TRAVELED OVERLAND TO WICK, and Citrine was forced to grit her teeth at the wagon's slow pace. She would've been much happier with the clothing and food she could stuff in a saddlebag, but Da would've been suspicious. In fact, she was even forced to wear one of the long, confining gowns he'd deemed suitable for marriage to the son of a powerful chieftain.

Bah.

At Wick, Citrine waited demurely with the wagon while William went to negotiate passage with a merchant vessel traveling north past Stroma, then west through the Minch to Lewes. It was galling, but much faster than traveling by land, especially through the MacKay lands.

When everything was arranged, Citrine oversaw the loading of her bags onto the birlinn, and even managed a smile as she said her goodbye to the Sinclairs.

I'll see ye soon.

William was the only one to stay with her. Da would've sent more men, but surprisingly, it was Dougal who spoke in her favor.

"She's a capable warrior," he'd said. "She can protect herself, but William will go along to help."

Citrine had peered suspiciously at the commander, surprised to hear him say anything complementary about her talent with a sword, but appreciative. Come to think of it, he'd always been in support of her marriage to a MacLeod… mayhap he was just anxious to get her on her way.

The first few hours at sea were exciting. The smells of the pitch mixed with the salt air and the bundles of wool wrapped in the space beneath the sailors' benches, soon became less than exotic. While the sails were down, the men lounged and told jokes, and after the wind died, they sang as they rowed.

William seemed right at home among them, even placing his small chest under a bench and taking his place at the oars. He was a likable sort of fellow, and Citrine was grateful he'd made friends, so he wouldn't be forced to only converse with her.

But it meant she knew no one, and after the novelty of sea travel wore off, she was bored.

Part of her was tempted to hike up her skirts and practice sparring with an imaginary opponent, even if her sword was buried deep in her trunk. But the knowledge that these sailors would undoubtably relate her conduct to the MacLeods of Lewes stayed her hand.

It wasn't that she cared what they thought, nay. But if they had no knowledge of her skills, they'd likely underestimate her. And she could use that.

So, she sat silently on one of her trunks under an awning in the rear of the boat. She'd kicked off her boots to better appreciate the roll of the deck beneath her, but with her gown draping elegantly to her feet, no one could see they were bare.

The captain—a slender man with a long, brown beard by the name of Angus Sinclair—sat near her and did his best to make polite conversation. It was clear he was more comfortable with the rough sailors but was trying to treat her the way a *lady* ought to be treated. He kept calling her *Lady Sinclair* and mentioning what an honor it was to carry one of the Sinclair Jewels on his vessel.

She managed not to roll her eyes at him.

By the second day, she'd exhausted all of her questions and

had learned more than she'd ever have thought about sailing a ship. The captain finally went back to his men and William.

Each night, the boat pulled ashore near a trading town, and they erected an elaborate camp for her. Despite her training, she rarely had to sleep out of doors, but discovered she still enjoyed it.

By the fourth day, Citrine was bored beyond measure. She'd even considered *embroidery* to pass the time, by the Virgin!

God's Wounds, send some excitement! Even another sea shanty!

In fact, a song would be interesting…she'd almost learned all of the verses to that one the men were singing yesterday about the lass with the loose bodice tie. She'd given up caring what the men would think of her bare feet, and had the gown hiked up to her calves to enjoy the cooler air while she watched the clouds chase each other over the cross spar.

She needed *some* kind of excitement! *Any kind!*

By midafternoon, it seemed as if she'd get her wish.

A sailor scurried over to the captain, pointing and speaking in a low tone. It was then that Citrine realized the feeling on the boat had changed; the men were no longer joking but sat straighter and seemed more alert. A few of them were fingering weapons and several were stealing glances to the left of the ship, where the mainland could occasionally be seen.

What is it?

It was a while before she could see the other ship, and another few minutes to realize *that* was what had everyone so distressed. Why? They'd seen a few merchant vessels on their voyage so far…isn't that what this was?

Like the sailors, she found herself watching the other ship closely, her fingers curling into the silk of her fine, green gown.

When the other ship changed directions and seemed to

turn toward them, the captain wasn't the only one who cursed —some louder than others—and began to mutter.

Citrine caught the word *pirates*.

She glanced at William and was surprised to see him staring at her thoughtfully. Thinking he was concerned for her, she gave him a quick nod to show him she would be fine. His lips curled up ever so slightly as he turned back to the approaching birlinn.

"Make ready! Weapons out, lads!" the captain called, reaching for his own sword. "If they mean to take us, they'll have a fight on their hands!"

It wasn't until that moment that Citrine truly understood what would happen.

A fight? With her sitting here in this stupid gown?

She stood and turned, wrestling open the lid to the trunk on which she'd sat. *Where is it?* She rifled through gowns and linen chemises, increasingly frantic.

Ah, there 'tis!

She breathed a sigh of relief as her fingers closed around the hilt of her short sword. As an afterthought, she grabbed the bag containing the first two Sinclair jewels and slung it over her head and shoulder, settling the leather in the small of her back.

There. If the boat *was* attacked, the pirates would not get the Sinclairs' most prized possessions.

Whirling, she was surprised how close the enemy ship had come. She bent her knees, settling into the ready position, and glanced at William. His sword was pointed at the deck as if he had no care for the oncoming threat and was smirking at her.

Smirking? Did he not think she could handle herself against a pirate attack?

She lifted her chin, determined to prove him wrong, and turned her attention back to the oncoming vessel.

Just in time to see the white of the sail obscured by a thick, black wool which was dropped in front.

The symbol of a pirate…but not just any pirate.

Citrine swallowed, not quite believing what she was seeing. She'd heard tales, aye, but no one above the age of seven truly believed them to be true. He was a myth, a legend of the North Sea…

Wasn't he?

Around her, the sailors began to curse or pray, and she knew this wasn't a myth or a legend.

The Black Banner was very real, and he was about to attack.

CHAPTER 4

Rory stood with one booted foot on the forward gunwale, his bared sword in his right hand and the knuckles of his left tight around the scabbard. He'd already donned the expensive, black kilt and now tensely watched the oncoming prize.

"Steady, lads," he called back to his crew. "We want her where she can't get away."

A murmur of "Aye, Captain" came from various mouths, but most knew their roles well enough to not need reminding.

Lifting his nose, he sniffed the air, knowing they were on the right track. Coming from the north like this, they'd steal their quarry's wind. The trick was to sail head-on, as if aiming for a collision, so that when Jock dropped the black sail and momentarily blocked their own sail, the birlinn would slow enough for both boats to survive.

He wanted their goods, not their lives.

He lifted his left hand, palm out, to indicate a slight course correction to Auld Marcus at the rudder. When he felt the vessel shift smoothly beneath his feet, Rory didn't bother hiding his smile.

This was where he excelled. This was what made him who

he was supposed to be. Here, on the sea, he knew exactly how to ensure things went his way. His family might think of him as the useless, youngest son, but not here.

He was the Black Banner.

Beside him, his second grunted quietly. "Ye think she's carrying aught good?"

Squinting against the reflection of the sun off the water, Rory shook his head. "Just a merchant. But hopefully on his way *back* from market, aye?"

Bull—named for the breadth of his shoulders—chuckled. "I cannae survive another trip to market, Banner."

Standing slightly behind Bull, Bartholomew clucked his tongue. "Ye made a piss-poor wool merchant, Bull. We'll no' ask ye to play that part again."

As this crew had gotten better over the years, they'd quit taking goods from merchants, because they were too much of a challenge to sell off. Now they hoped for jewelry or coins, although Rory had a sense of decency; he never took enough of a merchant's livelihood to force his children to starve, and rarely bothered to plunder the common sailors' sea chests.

His men would return to the Western Isles with enough coin to last through the winter, but not enough to become lairds.

"Nae wool," he agreed, his attention still on the approaching birlinn. "But I'm more interested in her stern. Who do ye think all that's for?"

There was an awning stretched across the rear of the boat, and he could see someone sitting there. A someone…and what looked to be a few chests.

"Passengers?" grunted Bull.

"Passengers mean baggage," Bartholomew speculated. "And baggage is much easier to dispose of."

Bull elbowed the older man. "Ye can have any of the fine tunics we find."

"I doubt that," Bartholomew snorted. "Jock will fight me for them."

"Ye'll get yer chance, soon enough," Rory cautioned, lifting his hand once more. "Ease ahead, Marcus!"

The ship was now in the perfect position.

"Are the lads ready?"

He waited for Bull to glance around. "Aye," he grunted. "Oars are boated, swords are out. We wait yer command, Banner."

"Excellent."

Rory eyed the other vessel, then darted a glance up at his own white sail. Their friend Jock was perched on the cross spar, a dirk in his hand and a gleam in his eye. He nodded his readiness.

It was always this moment when Rory's heart began to pound, that sense of anticipation washing through his veins. He knew his men felt it, too, and knew pulses were racing aboard their oncoming prize as well.

He judged their track and dropped his hand suddenly. "Come about, Marcus!" As the birlinn changed direction to come directly at the other boat, Rory dropped his foot to the deck, straightened, and called up to Jock, "Show them our banner!"

He could tell from the way the boat shuddered that Jock had no problem slicing through the lines which dropped the heavier black sail in front of the white one. It was done purely for theatrics, and was the reason behind his name.

It was their Black Banner.

With the bow of his birlinn pointed directly at the gunwales of the other boat, he lifted his sword. "Beware the black!"

Behind him, his men took up the cry: "Beware the black!"

When the two ships slammed together, he was the first over the side, but knew his men were behind him.

With a fierce sort of joy, he met the blades of the merchant ship's sailors, fighting his way toward the captain. His men were under orders not to kill indiscriminately. The Black Banner's reputation had never been bloodthirsty, and he wouldn't be the first one to change that.

Luckily, these men weren't warriors, and it showed. Of course, besides himself and Bartholomew, none of his own men had been trained as warriors either. But over their years on the Black Banner's crew, they'd learned.

These men weren't trained. A few cowered and prayed, while some met him fiercely with blades and cudgels. Rory knocked them all aside, leaping from one rower's bench to the next, intent on his prize: the captain.

But when he reached midship and could *see* the captain, Rory's aim changed. The captain was bellowing orders, his sword swinging madly even though none of the pirates were nearby. But it was the *passenger* who now held Rory's attention.

It was a woman, but not just any woman: a *lady*. She wore an expensive looking green gown and stood behind a traveling trunk.

He'd been right; passengers meant luggage. But a *lady* passenger meant *expensive* luggage.

His lips were already pulling up as he changed his grip on the hilt of his sword and swung to clear a path toward her. This one prize might be enough to return to Lewes; those trunks would contain costly gowns his men would give as gifts to wives and sweethearts, and a lady like her would have some valuables secreted away.

The knowledge of this raid's success had his blood pumping harder. "Beware the black!" he roared, and heard the cry being taken up behind him.

Wide-eyed, the woman backed further away. Her hands were by her sides, but her gaze never left him.

Bull was beside him now, bellowing like his namesake, reaching toward hapless sailors. The big man rarely used a blade, relying on his hands to do the necessary work. Rory didn't mind, because knocked heads were easier to recover from than sword wounds. It was tempting to let his friend deal with the captain…

Suddenly, there was only one more opponent between Rory and the woman; a young man who smiled mockingly and dropped his sword-point to the deck before stepping out of the way. He even made a little offering gesture to the lady, as if telling the pirate to have at her.

The lady—Rory was close enough now to see the sea air had torn off whatever covering she'd been wearing over her honey-gold hair—switched her gaze to the other man. "William!" she hissed angrily.

Not about to question the opportunity, Rory called to his second. "Bull, take the captain!" Rory twisted his body as he passed, making sure to keep the young man in sight in case the surrender was a ruse.

The man—William?—just grinned.

Rory held his sword in both hands, low in the ready position. Thank St. Ninian, because it meant he was able to raise it in time to block the next attack, which he absolutely hadn't been expecting.

He was still facing William when the sound of a blade whistling through the air alerted him to the danger, and he was lifting his even as he crouched and twisted. He caught the descending blade on his own and gaped at the wielder.

Which almost cost him his life.

The lady's sword was smaller than his, but she handled it with the skill and grace of someone who'd spent hours training. What she lacked in strength, she made up for in speed, and he was hard-pressed to match her attacks with his own blocks.

Of course, he'd figured this out by her third blow, and while he was certain he could've ended her attack, part of him didn't want to.

By all the saints, she was stunning.

Her hair was caught up in braids wound around her head, but plenty of it had come loose. The dark green of her bliaut was embroidered with gold at the neckline, and only served to accentuate the creamy tan of her skin.

Who was she?

Mayhap it was the shock, or mayhap the intrigue, which kept Rory from finishing the fight. He allowed her to attack again and again, not bothering to push her back while he caught her blows on the *forte* of his sword. He thought he might be able to stand there all day watching the determined tilt of her mouth and the way her pale eyes darted across him, looking for a weakness.

It was Bull's cry which wrenched Rory's attention back to the present.

"Banner!" It wasn't a call for help, but the signal the ship was theirs. "Black Banner!" Bull roared, and the rest of the pirate crew took up the cry.

And Rory knew, as much as he was enjoying the grace of the lady's attack, he had to end it.

He took a step, then another, forcing her back toward her chests, her blade ready in front of her and her gaze wary.

Offering her a grim smile, Rory raised his blade for a final attack, then jumped forward.

As expected, she jerked to the side, intent on catching his sword in hers. But the gown she was wearing wasn't made for sword battles, and her foot caught in the long skirt.

Her hip crashed into the trunk, and she rebounded toward him. He knocked her blade away as he reached out with his left hand and grabbed her around the middle, slamming her into his chest.

A moment of stillness caught them both, then her lips parted, and she sucked in a gasp.

His eyes fell to her mouth, and he was struck by the oddest thought. He couldn't recall ever seeing a more perfect pair of lips. They were as tanned as the rest of her, proving she spent time out-of-doors, but the lower one was twice as plump as the upper.

They were begging to be tasted.

It wasn't until she began to struggle that he realized how aroused he'd become in such a short amount of time. But rather than feel chagrined by his inability to keep control of his body, the thought sent another jolt of lust through him.

She'd felt his cock harden and had known what it meant.

Lifting his eyes to hers, he realized they weren't just a light brown, as he'd assumed before, but a topaz color which flashed in the sunlight.

That flash of anger was the only warning he got.

His own lips were pulling up on one side into a wry grin when she yanked her sword arm toward him, obviously intent on skewering him. He had to drop his sword to grab her wrist, because he damn well wasn't going to lose his hold on her any time soon.

She jerked again, but with one arm pinned between them and the other held tight in his grip, she couldn't do much harm. Or so he thought.

When he felt her shift her weight to lift one leg, he knew her intention. And *God's Blood*, why did that make him feel so amused? Instead of protecting his bollocks, he slid one foot forward—between her feet—and used it as leverage to lean forward. Trapped against him as she was, that put her off-balance, meaning she couldn't knee him.

He'd won.

"Hello," he said with a grin.

And she spat in his face.

Saints preserve him, but he started to laugh, which caused her to struggle harder, which made him more certain than ever: he wanted this woman.

Decision made, he loosened his hold on her, allowing her to pull away. But she only made it far enough that he could grip her other forearm in his right hand. Then it was a simple matter to pull them together and hold both of her wrists in one hand as he reached down to retrieve his sword.

Then, and only then, did he wipe her spittle from his cheek with a mocking nod.

The curse she spat at him had his brow raising, surprised a lady would know such language. Well, she'd proven to him yet again that she was not like the other ladies he'd known.

For a moment, staring down at his captive, yet still displaying defiance, he thought of his future wife. Would she be as beautiful as this hellcat? As spirited? She certainly wouldn't know how to knee a man in the bollocks—not a gentle daughter of a powerful Highland laird.

The spike of disappointment caught him by surprise.

Disappointment? Why?

Because Rory MacLeod's wife wouldn't be anything like this creature, and *this* was the kind of woman who should stand beside the Black Banner.

"Why do ye stare, whoreson? Have ye naught better to do?"

Purposefully, he took his time responding, dragging his gaze over her languidly, lingering on her breasts. He was an honorable man, aye, but a man nonetheless, and allowed all his desire into his expression.

When she sucked in another quick breath, he knew he'd alarmed her again.

"Why would I do aught else, lass? I've won yer ship, so the cargo is mine to do with as I see fit." He dropped his chin, making sure she saw the lecherous tilt of his lips. "*All* the cargo."

"I am no' *cargo*," she hissed. "I am a paying passenger. Release me!"

He pretended to consider it, although his mind had been made up. Whoever she was, she intrigued him. If he could tame her, convince her he was worth a tumble, they could both make the other very happy indeed.

"Nay, I think no'. Ye'll be coming with me."

With that, he turned his back to her, intent on his men. "Jock, see to it that—"

When she slammed into him from behind, he almost bit his tongue off. Damnation!

He whirled again, lifting her wrists and forcing her up on her toes. "See here, wench, this will go better for ye if ye dinnae anger me."

"I'm nae wench! Ye have nae right—"

"I'm a *pirate*. The Black Banner." With her off-balance like this, it was easy to pull her forward, causing her to stumble into him. "Treacherous and honorless. I can do as I wish, and if ye do no' cease yer struggles, I promise whatever ye're about to experience can be made much worse."

The color drained from her face, and in that moment, Rory felt like a true villain.

At least it shut her mouth.

He turned to Jock once more. "Ye ken what to take, lads. See to these chests as well." He knocked one booted heel against her luggage, knowing the *thump* indicated they were nice and full.

Scanning the conquered birlinn, he was pleased to see there didn't appear to be any dead, and his own men were moving about with minimal wounds. The captain was reluctantly turning over a pouch of coin to Bartholomew, the contents of which didn't look particularly heavy. The captured sailors were stretched out on benches, being tended to by their mates, or glowering angrily at Bull, who was the most intimidating of the guards.

The exception was William, the young man who had stood aside to allow Rory at the lady. The way she'd hissed his name had seemed...*disappointed?*

Now, the man stood with his arms crossed in front of his chest, a faint grin on his lips. *Why?* Why was he pleased with the outcome of this battle?

Or mayhap he wasn't. Mayhap he was just one of those men with an inappropriately wry sense of humor, who would smile at death.

Still, he seemed to be the one the lady knew, so Rory faced him directly.

"As for this *passenger*," he said, tugging the woman up against him, "she seems to hold the most value on board this vessel. We'll be taking her luggage...and *her*."

And damnation, but the man's smile grew.

"William!" The lady's frantic call was accompanied by another attempt to jerk out of Rory's hold. To go to him? Who was the young man to her?

"William, ye cannae do this!"

The man raised a brow in her direction.

"William!" she screamed. "Damn ye, and damn yer treachery. My father will ken—"

It was clear *William* wouldn't be fighting for her.

Rory lifted her with a grunt. It meant she was slung across his shoulders, because he wasn't going to loosen his hold on her wrists—the saints alone knew how she'd attack him then.

The position was awkward, but effective. All she could do was kick ineffectively and continue to curse William, albeit with less breath.

Her feet were bare.

He wasn't sure why the realization affected him, but he hadn't noticed it before. His *wife* wouldn't go around without shoes, likely she'd demand the finest slippers money could buy. But *this* firebrand…her feet might be bare, but she was using them—and her tongue—as much as possible.

So Rory was chuckling as he climbed atop one of the rower's benches and then up and over the gunwales. He turned.

"Jock, slice the sail lines. Bartholomew, I want all but four of those oars onboard by the time we shove off."

He wouldn't leave the conquered ship to flounder and sink, knowing he would be condemning the sailors to death. But without a sail and most of their oars gone, it would take a while for them to rally, and impossible to chase down Rory's own boat. He'd have Bull drop the oars overboard closer to shore, so the captain of the merchant ship could pick them up if he were lucky enough to find them.

When Rory received a nod from his men, he lifted a brow to Bull, who turned and bellowed to the crew. "Ye heard the Black Banner, men! Grab yer spoils, and let's catch some wind!"

As his men lifted their weapons in a cheer and began to rifle through her chests, Rory turned with his own struggling cargo.

She was kicking and calling him all sorts of interesting names, but that's not what caught his attention. Nay, it was the way her struggle had caused her braids to loosen, so they fell around his shoulder.

Aye, she was the most fascinating piece of plunder he'd ever taken, and he hoped he didn't live to regret it.

CHAPTER 5

PIRATES!

Citrine realized she was shaking as she huddled against one of the walls of the ship and watched her captors bustle about.

Their captain, the one who'd so easily overpowered her, had stomped aboard his birlinn and shrugged her off his shoulders. Determined to show him she wasn't beaten, she'd thrown herself at him, intent on scratching off his face if nothing else, but he'd had no trouble catching her wrists once more and tying them before her with a thin piece of braided rope.

Within moments, it seemed as if the pirates finished on the merchant vessel and had flowed back over the sides to their own ship. Some were carrying packets or bales of wool they'd stolen, and more than a few had her gowns draped over their dirty arms or shoulders.

She couldn't imagine what they planned to do with the gowns, other than sell them for the fabric, but she was surprised how little she cared. The clothing wasn't important to her in the first place; she'd only taken it so Da wouldn't suspect she intended to return to the Sinclair lands soon.

God's wounds, what would happen now?

She was tied up on the Black Banner's ship, getting farther and farther from the only people who knew anything about who she was, and her mission was in tatters. If she couldn't get to Lewes to search for the two missing jewels, she'd never be able to bring the brooch back to her father completed.

Thank the Blessed Virgin the pirates apparently hadn't seen the bag she still had slung over her shoulder—or had but didn't care to search it. The sapphire and agate—and the tapestry—were still nestled safe against her back, and she'd do absolutely everything in her power to keep them there.

Of course, the pirate captain had shown her that he could easily overpower her, which meant that the stones—and herself—weren't as safe as she'd like. If he could steal her from a Sinclair ship, claiming her as spoils of the battle the same way his men took coin and goods, then what did that mean?

It meant she—*and* the jewels—belonged to him now.

Oh God.

Damn William and his treachery!

Deciding it was better to stay angry than to think of her hopeless situation, she pushed herself into a sitting position, pulling her knees up, and hooked her bound hands around them. From this position, she could better see the pirates as they moved away from the helpless Sinclair ship.

Even by twisting around, she couldn't see her former vessel, and was almost glad for it. If she'd seen William smirking at her, she wasn't sure what she'd do. Why had he looked at her that way as she'd called for his help? Why had he just stood aside and let the pirate take her?

He was her *guard*. Granted, she's sparred with him enough to know she was as good a swordsman as he and didn't need his help. But as a Sinclair warrior, it was up to him to protect her. Instead, he'd practically *invited* the Black Banner to take her.

William Sinclair was either a coward or a traitor, and when she returned home, she'd make sure her father knew.

If I return home.

Nay, thinking like that did no good.

Surely not *everything* about the future was bleak? What were her assets?

The Black Banner had easily stolen her sword from her—it still rested on the deck of the other ship, presumably. Without her boots, she didn't have her dirk, either. In fact, in this ridiculous gown, she was completely without weapons... except her mind.

Aye, her mind wasn't as sharp as her twin's, but surely, she could think of a way out of this situation?

First, I need to ken why I'm here.

Why was she taken? Once she knew, she'd have a better idea of how to fight these pirates.

Aye, knowing what the Black Banner expected of her would—

When he stepped up on the raised deck in the stern of the ship, where she sat, she completely lost that thought.

He stopped and turned to the older man at the rudder. "Auld Marcus, go have a rest. I'll take over."

The older man nodded gratefully and waited until the Black Banner had stepped up to his spot, then scurried down the small ladder toward a wineskin hanging from the side of the boat.

Now would be the time to shove a dirk between his shoulder blades.

If only she had one.

When she sighed, probably more forlornly than intended, he glanced at her. One side of his lips twitched upward, and he raised a slightly mocking brow.

"Ready to admit defeat, wee firebrand?"

She was exhausted. Exhausted and beaten and helpless.

But she'd be damned if she let him know that.

She thrust her chin out. "Ready to release me, whoreson?"

He tsked and turned his attention to the front of the boat once more. "'Tis the second time ye insulted my mother. If I didnae have such an easy-going nature, that might merit punishment."

Punishment? Citrine swallowed, wondering what he could possibly do that was worse than he had done already.

Well, there was one thing, but she wasn't sure yet if that was his plan. Didn't pirates rape and pillage? Or was that the Norsemen? *Blessed Virgin*, but she was tired…her mind didn't seem to want to work properly.

Her chin sank to her knees, and she decided whatever he had planned for her, she wouldn't be foolish to prick his ire more than necessary.

For now.

Save yer strength, lass. For when it matters.

The hours dragged on, and Citrine's rear end went numb. She shifted her weight from side to side, pushing against the deck with her bare feet to take some of the pressure off her aching muscles. But she did her best not to move too much, not wanting to draw unwanted attention.

Occasionally, the Black Banner would glance at her, but he made no effort to engage her in conversation—taunting or otherwise. It was as if the pirates had forgotten she was there.

To her surprise, the pirates *sang*. Like…normal sailors. In fact, they did any number of things she'd seen the sailors on the Sinclair ship do: sing, bicker, climb the single mast with a speed she couldn't imagine, and challenge one another to contests of strength at the oars.

The only difference between these pirates and the sailors

on the other birlinn—besides the fact these were dressed all in black—was the mood. These pirates were almost *joyful*.

Because they just took a fine prize, ye ninny. Why would they no' be happy?

Their songs ranged from wistful to bawdy, and Citrine recognized a few of them from the men back home. Of course, her father would've never approved of her knowing the words, but she found herself humming under her breath to several.

Then there was the one she'd never heard before; one about treasure and battles and piracy. It seemed as if each verse was made anew by the man who stood from his bench to call it out, resulting in jeers or cheers, depending on the rhymes. Some verses were about the battle she'd just witnessed, and when the huge man who seemed to be second-in-command sang about her crossing swords with the captain —with plenty of double meanings—Citrine found herself blushing.

The refrain was simple, but the men roared it together.

"One of brown, and one of white,
And one of the deepest blue!
One glows gold in the fire's light,
Jewels in the hearthstone's view!"

To her surprise, the Black Banner even joined in, throwing his head back and laughing along with his men, obviously cheerful about the day's work.

He had a lovely voice, and why did she have to notice that?

In fact, he was lovely all over. *That* was something she'd seen right away, although she had been busy fighting him at the time.

He rested one hip against the side of the ship as he pushed easily against the long rudder, his strong legs encased in black boots. Above the simple black kilt, his stomach was flat and defined, and his chest...

Citrine swallowed and forced her gaze higher, to muscled shoulders and a strong jaw.

God forgive her, but she'd always been partial to a strong jaw.

His was covered in stubble a few shades lighter than the dark brown of his hair, which he kept cut short. He was younger than a pirate captain ought to be—at least one as notorious as he was. Come to think of it, she'd been hearing stories of the Black Banner since she was a girl, and this man couldn't be that much older than her, could he?

He was handsome, aright, and that was the problem.

From the moment she'd seen him, the moment she crossed swords with him, she'd known she could want this man. *Did* want him, wanted to feel him…but then he'd beaten her, taken her prisoner.

And now, no matter how handsome, how alluring, he would never have her.

It was almost twilight when he turned the ship toward shore. The men quieted, knowing their jobs well enough they didn't have to be told. They made landfall on an empty stretch of shoreline and worked together to pull the birlinn up on the sand and secure it, the process easier than she'd experienced the last few nights.

In fact, her escort had been taking her westward, toward Lewes. This pirate ship had been heading *away* from Lewes. Back toward home.

I can use that.

But when, without words, the Black Banner scooped her up and threw her over his shoulder once more, easily jumping down into the sand while carrying her, it was hard to hold on to that determination.

He carried her out of the sand to where the men were already lighting a fire and starting to cook, before easing her off his shoulder. It was…courteous of him?

"If I let ye loose, will ye run?"

She lifted her chin and met his eyes in the fading light. "If ye let me loose, I'll steal a dirk and slit yer throat."

To her surprise, he chuckled at her threat, shaking his head. "Fair enough. But I ken ye have to relieve yerself afore the night, aye?"

All afternoon, she'd watched the men piss over the side of the ship, not caring at all for privacy. The knowledge this man had not only thought of her comfort, but something so intimate, brought an immediate flush to her cheeks.

"I thought so," he chuckled. "Come."

Before she could object, he'd wrapped a large hand around her bindings and tugged her toward the nearby wood. As she stumbled along behind him, her bare feet crunching on twigs and last year's leaves, he called over his shoulder.

"Stay in yer black, lads. We have a visitor!"

The series of groans behind her had Citrine's eyes opening wider with an important realization.

Stay in yer black. It meant that, after an attack, the men were used to changing out of the pirate costumes. The Black Banner was concerned that whatever they changed *into* would reveal their real identities.

And he didn't want that.

So, who was he really?

That line of thought came to a crashing halt when he pulled her into the wood and reached for her wrists. Pulling a small dirk from his belt, he sawed through the rope near the knot, then tucked the weapon back where it belonged.

Her attention was on the weapon so long—wondering what would need to be done to pull it from his belt and use it against him—she didn't notice he was rubbing at her wrists until the tingling in her fingers started. She stared down at her hands, lips slightly parted.

He was being *courteous*? Not only that, his touch, where his callused fingers were massaging at her stiff wrists, was causing an odd warmth to race up her arm.

Flustered, she tugged away from him.

He, of course, tugged right back, causing her to stumble against him. He lifted a brow in challenge.

"Can I trust ye to piss without being tied, lass? If ye're planning on running, I'll tie ye and damn the inconvenience."

God's wounds, she wanted to run! But her body's needs were greater.

Thrusting her head high, she met his eyes with a mulish glare, and gave her arm another yank. This time, he let her go, and she turned to stalk to a nearby tree she could lean against as she squatted.

Although her back was to him, she could feel his gaze on her as she lifted her skirts to perform the necessary deed. It was humiliating.

But he'd rubbed her wrists.

And why did that make her feel...tingly?

Before she'd even stood completely, he was there again, reaching for her wrist, tugging her away from the tree. She expected him to lead her back to camp, but he didn't.

Instead, he halted under a large birch and spun her around. Startled, she didn't realize what he was doing until after he'd grabbed her other hand and was tying her wrists together behind her back.

That's when she started to struggle, but it was too late. Her hands were secure in the most awkward way possible. There was no way she'd be able to fight him like this.

Panicking now, she lurched forward, but was halted when he grabbed her bound wrists. The jolt sent a pain up her shoulder, and she hissed aloud.

And he cursed. "By all the saints, lass, cease or ye'll hurt yerself further!"

It was the regret in his tone which stopped her more than anything else.

Barefoot in the dirt and detritus of the woods, she held her breath as he came around to face her. For a long moment, he said nothing, just stood there looking at her, and she'd never felt so naked.

Aye, she was clothed, but with her hands behind her back like this, her breasts were thrust forward, and his gaze definitely lingered on them.

She swallowed, wondering if this was the moment she'd been dreading. Was *this* the reason he'd taken her?

Before she could ask, he stepped forward, bringing their chests much closer. He made no move to ravish her, but the anticipation—the fear—had her heart pounding and made her throat dry.

Without lifting a hand, he leaned forward, his lips near her ear. His stubbled jaw scraped against her cheek, but rather than hurting her, it was a deliciously intimate sort of feeling.

What in damnation?

Why was her body reacting this way?

"Ye're a beautiful woman, lass," he whispered in her ear. "I would have ye for my own, but ye're a firebrand."

It took her two tries to get her voice to work, but she didn't pull back. She just straightened her shoulders and stared ahead, not daring to move for fear her body would betray her by swaying *toward* his heat.

"A—Aye, a firebrand who'll never join with ye, Banner."

A brush of warm air against her ear sent a shudder through her, and she realized it had been a chuckle. "Nay, I suppose ye wouldnae. I'd hoped to be able to convince ye otherwise, but tying ye up was likely no' the right kind of convincing, was it?"

She was surprised he was willing to admit his mistakes and this time, *did* pull back enough to meet his eyes. "Ye want me willing?"

His brow twitched, and in the failing light, she saw he had dark blue eyes, a shade darker than her sister Saffy's. "Aye, lass." And *that's* when he lifted one hand to her cheek and dragged the back of his finger down to her jaw. "'Tisnae fun if both parties arenae enthusiastic."

"A dishonorable man wouldnae care," she carefully pointed out to keep herself from thinking how his touch had made her shiver.

He dropped his chin in acknowledgement. "And whatever I am, I am honorable."

I am honorable.

Relief made her knees weak. He didn't intend to rape her.

But she had to know… "What will ye do with me?"

To her surprise, he blew out a breath and stepped away from her, running his hand through his hair. "I dinnae ken. 'Twas likely a mistake to take ye."

That was such an unexpected admission, a startled laugh burst out of her.

"Aye," he said with a shrug. "But a hopeful cock makes many a poor decision."

It sounded like the truth. A little more hopeful now, she twisted slightly to show her bound hands. "Will ye let me go?"

In a flash, he was upon her once more, close enough she could reach out and knock her head against his.

Or kiss him.

She squeezed her eyes closed on that thought. *She* was tired. That was the only explanation for how her emotions had been jumping around since he'd pulled her off the ship.

"Lass," he said in that quiet murmur. "I cannae let ye go."

His words should've caused despair, but all she was focused on was the scent of him—salt and leather and hemp. With her eyes closed like this, her entire *world* became the knowledge he was so close, and oh-so-touchable.

"I ken ye, lady. If I untie ye, ye'll do yer best to kill me afore ye run."

I ken ye.

It was a disturbing and somehow exciting thought. She shuddered and opened her eyes. "I'll no'. I swear." Did she sound as if she was pleading? Did it matter? "If ye cut me loose, I'll run, and never tell a soul I saw ye."

He cocked his head, but it was hard to read his expression in the failing light. "Ye're a MacKay then? We're on their land or close enough ye could get help and return to make us rue our actions."

Rue his actions? God help her, all she wanted now was to retrieve her sword and take the jewels back home.

Home? Nay, she had to get to Lewes to find the remaining jewels. *Then* she could return home. But aye, her father was allied with the MacKays; she'd be able to find help here.

"Please?" she whispered, hating herself for it.

And from his wince, he knew how much it had cost her to say it.

"Turn around, lass," he said.

Eagerly, she did, whirling to offer him her bound hands. But after he untied her, he only held her long enough to turn her back around and bind her wrists in front of her once more, albeit less tightly than before.

When he met her gaze, she saw an apology there. "I cannae risk my men, lass."

He wasn't letting her go.

But he wasn't going to rape her either.

With her hands tied in front of her, she was a little less helpless and felt a bit more in control. When she'd stood in front of him with her hands behind her back, she'd felt like a piece of goods on display in a market stall, eager to catch someone's eye.

And why had that feeling made her throat go dry and a secret flood of warmth to spill between her thighs?

With a sigh he probably hadn't meant her to hear, he tugged her forward by her hands, and she followed dully, done trying to analyze her reaction to this man.

But when she stepped on a sharp stick in the near-darkness, she sucked in a hissing breath, unable to stop the reaction to the pain.

He whirled, his hand dropping to his hilt, before his quick gaze took in the problem. "By the saints, lass!" He lifted her skirts just enough to reveal her bare feet, then cursed quietly.

Before she knew his intentions, he'd bent and grabbed her behind her knees. When he straightened, she gave a little yelp of alarm as he lifted her effortlessly.

He didn't look down at her but kept his gaze straight ahead. She pulled her hands up to her chest, not sure if she should be fighting his hold or not, and gazed at the muscles working in his jaw.

Just as they reached the circle of firelight and could hear his men making merry, he stopped. He still didn't look at her when he finally said, "I'll find ye some shoes."

It wasn't an apology, but the knowledge he cared for her discomfort sent another flood of surprising emotions through her chest.

'Tis likely just exhaustion.

Surely that explained the haze in which she found herself, sitting beside the fire as she gobbled up the bread and cheese someone offered her, and even taking a few swigs from the wineskin the withered man who'd been at the rudder offered her.

She sat and watched the men taunt one another, some drunk and some not, until Banner stood and called out assignments for the watch. Struggling to her feet, she caught his surprised glance, before something changed in his eyes.

"Come with me, lass," he said gently and led her toward the edge of the firelight, ignoring a few hoots and bawdy jeers from his men.

She stiffened, not sure what to expect.

I am honorable.

Reminding herself of his words did help, and when he laid out a plaid—impossible to tell the pattern in the darkness—and tugged her down to it, she was almost certain she'd be safe enough to sleep.

But as tired as she was, when he rolled onto his side and tugged her up against him, fitting her arse against his erection, she couldn't sleep. She knew what he was feeling, knew what he wanted, but he wasn't acting on it.

I am honorable.

Finally, she forced herself to close her eyes, to pillow her head on her bound arms and relax. More of her back touched him then, but it couldn't be helped.

"Go to sleep, lass," came his deep rumble beside her ear, his voice feathering the hairs on the back of her head. "I'll keep ye safe."

On that promise, she obeyed his command and fell into an exhausted slumber.

CHAPTER 6

IT WAS the first time Rory had woken up with a woman in his arms, and he discovered he didn't mind it at all.

Since becoming a man—and mayhap a little before that—he'd taken his pleasure where it was offered. That meant he'd never had occasion to spend the night with a woman and had always assumed his wife would be the first.

But this lass…What was her name? Last night, among the trees, he'd come so close to kissing her, he could *taste* it. And although she held herself apart, although she told him an emphatic *nay*, there was something about her which hinted at a *mayhap*.

He blew out an exasperated breath, careful to keep quiet and not disturb her.

Honorable, he reminded himself. The lass had said *nay*, so he'd respect that. But he couldnae just release her, not here. They'd camped in this spot before, and he knew they were miles from the closest village. She'd likely get lost and die in the wilderness as find help…and that was if she didn't attack him first.

Nay, he'd keep her safe—and tied—until they reached

Durness. He could release her near enough for her to walk to town, and by the time she raised the hue and cry, he and his men would be long gone.

Instinctively, his arms tightened around her, surprised at the disappointment the idea of letting her go brought him.

Mayhap I'm turning into a real pirate, eh?

She stirred and murmured, her cheek pillowed against his shoulder, and her arms resting beside his hip. Sometime during the night, she'd rolled over, and he'd been glad for it. That bag she carried had been poking him while he laid there holding her, unable to sleep, and this position was much more comfortable.

So much so that, when Jock had come to wake him for his watch, he'd shaken his head.

"Sorry, friend," he'd whispered, "but I'll have to keep watch from here."

Jock had chuckled, but Rory spoke the truth. The lass was exhausted, and he'd not disturb her further. He kept watch from his back, his arm around her.

Glancing over at her, he was surprised to see her eyes open, although she didn't look totally awake yet.

"Good morning," he murmured. "How do ye feel?"

"Safe."

Her eyes widened at her confession, as if she hadn't meant to say the word, and he pretended not to notice the telling slip. Instead, he sat up, pulling her upright as well.

"Let us be on our way then."

She didn't speak again as he led her into the woods to perform her morning necessities, nor as his crew handed over hard bread to break her fast. She followed him down to the beach quietly enough and allowed him to lift her over the gunwale, so Bull could reach under her shoulders and pull her up the rest of the way.

She even settled into her place from yesterday in the stern, beside the rudder.

Rory wasn't sure how he felt about that; her having "a place" on his ship meant she was beginning to belong, and it was clear she'd murder him if given the chance.

He and the other men shoved their shoulders against the clinker-built bow of the birlinn and pushed it out into the water. Offering his hands as a perch, he and two others helped most of the men aboard.

Then he and the other two stripped out of their kilts, tossing them up onto the bow as they shoved the vessel into deeper water. The water was warmer here than Lewes, but not by much. Still, it was as invigorating as always.

And when, with a grunt, he hoisted himself up by the line Bull had dropped for them, Rory couldn't help but notice the way *she* was staring at his bare arse.

He was grinning as he wrapped his kilt around himself once more and took the rudder.

Once they were far enough from land, he called Auld Marcus back to his post as steersman and crossed the deck to crouch beside her. She was sitting cross-legged today, her bare feet tucked under her dress, her bound hands in her lap, and her gaze merely curious.

Safe.

That's what she'd said this morning. He suspected it wasn't so much that she wasn't used to being safe, but that she was used to providing for her own safety. Who *was* this woman?

With her staring back at him, he settled on his heels and enjoyed watching her. She was beautiful, aye, but his sisters were beautiful women, too. What was it about her which was so tempting?

She has Charlotte's spirit.

Aye, that was it. This lass was no meek lady, content to sit quietly and become a powerful laird's wife. She was nothing like his sisters or his future wife. His wife, who'd agreed to shackle herself to him, the youngest son of a laird, in the hopes of an alliance with his father.

This woman was no pawn.

Between their battle yesterday and the night on the ground, her braids had come completely undone, and now her honey-blonde hair hung in snarls around her shoulders. Reaching out one hand, he tugged a twig from the rat's nest and flicked it away, surprised she didn't lean away from his touch.

Instead, her light brown eyes followed his move. Light brown? Nay, that didn't do them justice. Here in the sun, they shone topaz. *Gold*, even.

Her lower lip was still just as tempting, and her freckles still made him want to taste her.

"What will ye do with me?"

Her voice, low and private, jerked him out of his musing. "What?"

"Yesterday, ye told me ye were honorable and wouldnae rape me. Last night, ye kept me safe. But now, the way ye're looking at me tells a different story."

Chagrined, he rocked back on his heels and shoved a hand through his short hair. *Honorable.* Aye, he was.

In one swift move, he stood, then tugged her to her feet. It was clear from the way she wobbled that she hadn't expected the move, and he relished the chance to hold her arm a bit too long.

When she was steady, he reached for the dirk at his belt. If he'd been wearing his boots, he would've used the smaller one he kept there, but he'd never pulled them back on after his morning swim.

Sure, she was watching him intently, so he kept his attention on her hands as he sawed through the hemp fibers, then picked the line away from her skin. This time, though, instead of rubbing her skin to ensure the circulation was back, he flipped the dirk over and offered it to her, hilt-first.

She was rubbing at her own wrists and glanced up at him, surprise evident in her eyes. "Why?"

Unsure himself, he shrugged. "I'll no' dishonor ye, lass. We're too far from land for ye to escape afore I'm ready to let ye go, and if ye do me harm, ye *have* to ken my men will no' be happy." He shoved a hand through his hair again. "So, take it."

Frowning now, she didn't ask again, but flicked it around in her fingers and tucked it through the decorative, braided belt that hung low on her hips. The weapon looked out of place with her gown…but not out of place in her hands.

This was the start of a hesitant truce.

The day progressed with the birlinn tacking back and forth to take advantage of the winds pushing them northeastward. They passed by two potential prizes, but none of them questioned Rory's decision to make for Durness without delay.

She began to ask him questions about the ship, and he settled beside her on the aft deck to answer. He even made her chuckle once or twice and was impressed by the depth of her knowledge and intelligence.

And he still didn't know her name.

"And why is it most of yer men sit idle now, Banner?"

Banner. She didn't know his name, either, and it was most definitely for the best.

"The wind is steady today, and we're moving fast enough." He pointed to the expanse of white wool which was luffing for the briefest of moments before it caught the wind again as they came about. "Every man aboard keeps one eye on the sail, for if it fails or the wind dies, they'll be back to rowing in nae time."

"And is rowing as efficient?"

He chuckled. "No' nearly, but with enough strong backs, we can overtake aught."

Mayhap it was the reminder they weren't sailors but *pirates*, which had her shifting uncomfortably. "And I assume we're turning back and forth like this to catch the wind?"

"Aye." He was grateful for the change in topic. "'Tis called *tacking*, and the only way to sail against the wind as we are now."

They were sitting on the edge of the aft deck, their feet dangling over the storage area below, level with the heads of the men on the benches. Rory leaned back on one hand and reached for the pouch on his belt with the other. It was second nature to pull out the pearl to roll it between his knuckles while he spoke.

"The square sail is powerful, see? I've heard of some birlinns with sails in the shape of triangles, but *true* power would come from a second sail." With the hand holding the pearl, he gestured toward a spot forward of the mast. "A second mast there with another sail. And deep sides"—he waved toward the gunwales—"to protect from boarders like us. A deep keel, mayhap, although 'twould make it impossible to beach effectively. And—och, never mind."

He turned to her with a wry grin, a little embarrassed to be caught spouting his ideas for a new class of ship, but it died when he saw her expression.

She wasn't even listening to him, he'd wager. Her attention was focused entirely on the pearl in his hand, and unconsciously, he tightened his fingers into a protective fist around it.

Her hand darted out, and to his surprise, strong fingers wrapped around his wrist as she yanked his fist toward her. Unbalanced, he almost toppled into her, and the knowledge their positions were reversed from yesterday made his lips twitch, even as he lifted a brow in question.

"Lass?"

Her other hand was scabbling at his fingers, and he loosened his hold enough for her to pry them open and reach for the pearl. He made a swipe for it, but she was faster, and scrambled to her feet before he could stop her.

Genuinely worried now, he hopped to his feet and lunged for her, but she darted out of the way. Instead, his hand closed around the material of her sleeve, and when he tugged, her gown pulled a bit, revealing one creamy shoulder to the sunshine.

She didn't notice; her attention was entirely on the pearl she held between two fingers.

He moved closer, not wanting to startle her into dropping or throwing the precious jewel, but knowing she couldn't get away from him.

"Lass?"

"Where did ye get this?" she asked in a hoarse whisper. "Where?" When she lifted her eyes to his, he saw fury and intelligence and recognition in them.

She kens this stone.

It was his first thought, and with a certainty he hadn't expected, he knew it was the right one.

Why would she recognize the stone?

Without answering her, he shifted his hold from her sleeve to her hand and turned to his men.

"Bull!" His call traveled over whatever conversations and songs the men were engaged with and caught their attention. "Did any of ye—the ones who went through the lady's chests— find any jewels? Stones of any kind?"

Some of the crew shook their heads, but others scrambled for their own bags and chests under their benches. Three men held up jewelry, two necklaces, and a jeweled belt. They didn't look anything like his pearl, but he gestured to Bull to bring them up, not wanting to let go of her.

"These are yer things?" he growled as Bull held them up.

When Rory glanced her way, she pressed her lips together

and stared daggers back. He then shook his head to Bull, letting his second know he could return the jewelry to the men who'd stolen it for themselves or their sweethearts.

Rounding on her, he lifted her hand—not the one with the pearl. "Ye ken that stone. Why? How? Do ye have its match?" He'd long wondered about the pearl's origins and how it came to be in his mother's headboard. Did this lady know the answer to the mystery? "What are ye hiding?"

She was good. Verra good. He wouldn't have guessed her secret had she not lowered her lashes just a fraction when he'd said the word *hiding*.

But what?

The satchel!

With a curse, he dropped her hand and reached for the leather satchel she'd kept snug against her body since yesterday's attack. She tried to twist to stop him, but with the pearl in her hand, was unable to prevent him from yanking the strap over her head and down one arm. She grabbed at the bag then, but not enough to prevent Rory from tearing it open.

A box! A small wooden box.

With a triumphant glance her way, he wrenched the lid open.

"Nay! Please—"

She bit down on the plea with a noise not unlike a sob, but Rory's attention was caught by the contents.

Two pouches rested atop a folded tapestry. He lifted a pouch and poured the jewels out.

An agate, as big around as his thumb, shined up at him. Hurrying now, he dumped the other pouch over, revealing a large sapphire whose facets caught the afternoon sun. Both were smooth on one side, as if they'd been set into a piece of jewelry like his pearl.

Sucking in a pleased breath, he glanced at her with a raised brow. She was staring, stricken, down at the jewels.

"Ye ken exactly how to please a pirate, lass," he crooned.

Slowly, she shook her head, reaching for the box with the hand holding the pearl. He lifted it out of her reach and tsked quietly.

"Ye've been keeping secrets."

Swallowing, she turned anguished eyes to him. "Ye said ye were honorable." Her chin jutted out mulishly, and the look in her eyes slowly turned to anger. "Ye said ye were *honorable*."

"Aye," he taunted, knowing he'd rather have her angry than distraught. "But that was about the matter of yer body. Yer verra, verra fine body." He made a point of dragging his approving gaze to her tits and back up again. "This is about *jewels*."

Her eyes flashed with golden fire, but she swallowed against. "They're *mine*."

He grinned. "No' anymore."

"Ye bastard!" she hissed, jerking her wrist fruitlessly. "Ye whoreson! Give them back!"

"Nay." When she was livid at him, she was a formidable opponent. But if he allowed her to turn anguished eyes on him again, he knew himself well enough to know he'd lose out on these magnificent jewels which matched his pearl. "I'll no' give them back willingly." An idea came to him. "But mayhap a trade…"

He kept his expression carefully blank, wondering what she would offer in exchange.

St. Ninian, let it be a kiss. He'd been aching to taste her since the first time their blades clashed.

"A trade?" she spat, her fist tight around the pearl. "How about ye give me back my jewels, and I dinnae kill ye?"

Ignoring her threat, he allowed his eyes to flick down to her fist. "And my pearl? Ye'll return it in the bargain?"

"Nay!" She shook her fist under his nose, her hair—which

she'd attempted to tame—whipping around her head. "'Tis no' yers. Ye stole it!"

He jerked back, his mouth open to form a denial before his brain caught up.

Easy, lad. She kens ye're a pirate, aye? 'Tis natural.

Taking a deep breath, he dropped his chin to meet her gaze directly. "Lass, I'll ignore the insult, because I ken why ye'd think that. But I swear on my niece's soul that I did no' steal that jewel. It belongs to my family."

She was not distracted from her ire by his vow. "Lies! It belongs to *my* family."

Rory's brows rose. Her family? Was it possible this lass was a MacLeod? His eyes darted over her features, trying to remember…

Nay, he'd remember someone as bonny as her. She was no MacLeod.

"'Tis mine," he said simply, holding out his hand. "Return it."

She lifted her chin. "Ye return *my* jewels."

He shook his head, enjoying the fire in her eyes. "Pirate, lass. Remember?"

Suddenly, all the fight seemed to drain out of her with a sound between a sigh and a sob. Her fist tightened around the pearl and she reached for the box, only to halt a distance away.

Her fingers trembled.

"Please," she whispered. "I need them."

Need them?

How intriguing.

"What would ye do for them, my wee firebrand?" he asked quietly.

She swallowed again, then met his eyes. "Anything," she breathed.

Anything? Rory forced himself to breathe, trying to control the way his cock jumped under his kilt and his fingers itched to reach for her.

He licked his lips. "Anything?" He tried for nonchalance, but knew he'd failed.

"Aye," came her strangled agreement. "Anything."

By all the saints and sinners! These jewels meant so much to her?

Rory snapped the box shut, the sound loud enough to startle her.

"Ye have yerself a deal, lass." He *would* taste her lips.

She nodded. "But please…no' here." Her eyes flicked over his shoulder to the crew, who were likely watching the drama unfolding with interest. "No' with them watching."

His brows rose slightly. She didn't want his crew watching him kiss her? Well, she wouldn't be the first to demand privacy. He was about to acquiesce when she glanced up at him.

The look she turned on him wasn't anguish. It wasn't anger. It was…resignation.

Defeat.

And with that look, he knew he'd won. God forgive him, because he knew he wouldn't be able to forgive himself for breaking her this way.

CHAPTER 7

ANYTHING.

This time, it was Citrine who took his hand and led him away from his men when they made landfall. It was still early afternoon, but Banner hadn't immediately made for shore after her agreement. Instead, he'd been searching for a specific type of beach—secluded enough, she supposed, for a pirate crew to land.

And once they did, he called out assignments to specific sailors. The large man, called Bull, was in charge of the group who stripped down and swam out to inspect the hull in the shallows. Jock—the wiry, dark-haired man—gathered a few men to check the seams in both sails. And Bartholomew led a hunting party up the steep cliffs which bordered the beach.

Then, Black Banner turned to her with a quirked brow and said, "Time for ye to fulfill yer end of the bargain, lass."

Bargain. Such an innocent word for what she'd just promised. Trading her body for the jewels…

But it was worth it. *Anything* was worth retrieving all of the Sinclair jewels and giving her father and her clan a future.

So, she was the one to take his hand, trying to ignore the warmth that shot up her arm from his touch.

I would have privacy.

He'd granted her that much by landing ashore, but she would go farther.

Of course, there'd be no sun-dappled meadow or burbling brook here, nay. This was a rocky beach, bordered by the sea on one side and harsh cliffs on the others. There *were* trails here and there, proving there were humans nearby, but it was a beautiful location.

It matters naught. Ye'll have yer eyes closed.

Would she though? Or was the thought of giving herself to this man not as bad as she might've once thought? She was no blushing virgin, and she knew how to bring herself to pleasure. So, she knew what it meant when her body reacted this way to Banner; her heart seemed to pump faster, her palms itched to touch him, and a heaviness settled between her legs, urging her to press against his hardness.

Following along behind her, he said nothing, but still carried her pouch with the jewels and box in one hand. And she still clutched the pearl.

When this trade was done, she'd negotiate for the pearl.

And for the information about its origins.

All she could imagine was that it had been on Lewes this whole time, mayhap in the MacLeod family's possession, and the Black Banner attacked one of them to steal it.

But he'd sworn on his niece's soul he hadn't stolen it, sworn it belonged to his family.

And he'd been intense enough, so Citrine believed him.

Was he a MacLeod, then?

"I think this is the best ye're going to get, lass. Unless ye want to walk all the way to Durness?"

When he tugged her gently to a stop, she looked around. A large outcropping hid them from the rest of the crew, and there was no one up the beach. She glanced about, but saw no evidence of watchers above either.

He was observing her with a smirk and a twinkle in his blue eyes. "Ye didnae drag me out here to stab me, did ye? 'Twould be perfect with all this privacy ye insisted on."

Citrine bristled, as it honestly hadn't occurred to her. "I am honorable."

They were his words and the only defense she would offer. She *would* honor this bargain.

He nodded, mayhap hearing the unspoken meaning. "As am I," he said as he dropped the pouch into the sand beside his feet and held out his hand. "The pearl, please."

Please. He didn't have to say that. She swallowed and then forced her fingers to uncurl. He snatched it from her hand and lifted it in a little salute, then dropped it into a pouch on his belt.

When he straightened once more, he cleared his throat, and she suddenly realized he was finding this as awkward as she was. Why? Did he not ravish women on a regular basis? Is that not what pirates did?

I am honorable.

If she was going to make this bargain, it would be on her terms.

Lifting her chin, she met his eyes and reached for the laces under her arm.

A look of confusion flashed in his eyes, but when her gown sagged off her shoulder, his gaze dropped to the skin revealed, and his tongue darted out across his lower lip.

Be daring, lass.

She *could* do this.

When she lifted her arms to him invitingly, she managed to hold her gown up as well. He needed no further urging, but closed the distance between them in a heartbeat. His large hands settled on her hips, and he pulled her snug against him, her pelvis cradling the hardness beneath his kilt.

"Are—are ye sure about this, lass?" he asked in a rough whisper.

Her hands rested on his shoulders, in a position which shouldn't have felt so natural. "Aye," she whispered, meeting his blue gaze.

And in that moment, she *was* sure. If he wasn't a pirate, and she wasn't his captive, and the ownership of the jewels wasn't between them…she'd be *verra* sure. He was a gorgeous, well-built man, and he made her tingle with excitement and lust.

She knew she wouldn't regret this afternoon.

So, she offered herself to him. "Take me, Banner."

With a groan of surrender, he lowered his lips to hers, and she freely accepted his kiss.

Blessed Virgin, but he could kiss! She was no novice, but not verra experienced either. William had been the last to thrust his tongue—

Nay, dinnae think of that treacherous coward now.

Instead, she sighed against Banner's lips and gave herself over to the sensations. When he sensed her surrender, he wrapped one arm around her back, not only pressing her even closer, but accepting some of her weight when her knees suddenly wobbled.

His tongue teased her lips until they parted, and his first foray seemed almost hesitant. She gladly opened more and proved she could meet him head-on. He groaned again, and she found herself wrapping her arms around his neck.

Forget their *bargain*! This was for her pleasure!

When he pulled his lips from hers, she gasped, feeling as if it was the first time she'd breathed since he'd touched her. But to her delight, he didn't leave her, but moved his lips to her jaw, then her neck.

Citrine allowed her head to fall back, presenting a better

angle for his kisses. And when his mouth trailed across her shoulder, she surged up on her toes as if offering herself to him. Using his hold on her waist, he took the hint and lifted her higher, so he could taste the skin below the neckline of her gown.

It was then that his other hand moved, his rough palm catching on the material of her bliaut before it closed around her left breast. She sucked in a gasp as pure pleasure darted from his touch to her pelvis.

"By the Virgin, *aye!*" she whimpered, arching into his touch with a moan.

It was all the encouragement he seemed to need. Banner tugged at her gown with two fingers and bared the breast he'd been fondling.

The salty air caressed her bare skin, but that wasn't why she shivered. Nay, it had more to do with the knowledge he wanted to bed her, and soon the magnificent member she felt straining against his kilt would be *inside* her.

And then she wasn't thinking at all, because his lips fastened around her nipple and she bucked against him, the erotic sensation causing a flood of warmth between her legs.

"Banner!" she panted. "*Please.*"

When his tongue gave one last swirl and he pulled away from her breast, she almost moaned in disappointment. But his hand covered her once more, and he lifted his lips to hers.

This kiss was more urgent, and she couldn't help but compare the thrusting of his tongue to what she *wanted* him to be doing. In that moment, Citrine cared naught for who might see them, or the fact she didn't know this man's real name. She was ready to throw herself to the sand and lift her gown for him.

And mayhap she would have had he not pulled away at that moment, his gasp proving he didn't want to sever their connection any more than she did.

But he didn't kiss her again.

Instead, he lowered his forehead to hers, his breaths coming as fast and as heavy as hers, as he loosened his hold and allowed her to slide back to solid footing. The friction from his hardness caused her to shudder.

He tucked her breast back into her gown and pulled the material up to her shoulder, anchoring it in place with a heavy hand which clearly wanted to be elsewhere.

She might've encouraged him to touch her again, but her mind was foggy, in a haze from the passion he'd just evoked with nothing other than his lips and a few caresses.

"By St. Ninian, lass," he finally croaked, his eyes still squeezed shut. "I am sorry."

She reared back, severing their connection. "Sorry?"

He shook his head slightly and winced. "I shouldnae have pushed ye…"

When he swallowed and opened his eyes, she saw regret and something else in his gaze, and understanding came crashing over her.

She'd been willing to bed this man…and all he'd wanted was a kiss. He was *apologizing* for going further than a kiss, when she would've allowed him much, much more.

And not just in exchange for the jewels.

I am honorable.

The reminder of her words caused her to nibble on her lower lip. He *was* honorable. Who had heard of an honorable pirate?

He groaned again and dropped his forehead to hers once more. "Damnation, my wee firebrand. When ye do that, I want to taste ye again."

Chewing on her lip, Citrine considered her options. She *could* respond with something saucy, inviting him to do just that. But then she'd become little more than another conquest of the great Black Banner.

Better to end it here.

"Firebrand?"

"Aye," he croaked. "When the light hits yer eyes, they glow like fire. Did ye ken it?" With a shrug, he straightened. "Golden fire."

Citrine stared, trying to remember if anyone had ever said anything nearly that wonderful to her before.

His hand slid from her back to her hip once more, and his other hand fell from her shoulder to her arm, then her hand, and he squeezed it.

"Thank ye, wee firebrand. The jewels are yers once more."

Just like that?

"But…"

Ah, there is *more.* She lifted a brow.

He cleared his throat and began again. "But if there's ever aught I can do to convince ye to allow me a tumble, I hope ye'll tell me. That was…" He blew out a breath and shook his head. "But I dinnae even ken yer name."

"Nor I yers," she was quick to point out.

His lips twitched. "Aye, but ye're no' a notorious pirate, are ye? With a reputation to protect?"

So, he admitted to hiding his real identity and that of his men? It would explain why he and his crew were still wearing black despite the danger of being found at their camp and being accused of being pirates.

As far as this adventure was concerned, he was the Black Banner, and that's how she would remember him once she was able to escape. The Black Banner, a surprisingly honorable pirate who kissed like an angel and made her feel like a devil.

But there was no reason for him not to know who *she* was.

So, she lifted her chin and met his eyes. "My name is Citrine."

However, she might've imagined him taking the news, it wasn't this way.

His nostrils flared as if he'd smelled something foul, and he jerked back, *away* from her. When his hands left her, she almost followed him, so disappointed was she.

But the look of horror on his face stopped her.

"Citrine?" he repeated in a rasp. "Citrine *Sinclair*?"

When she nodded mutely, wondering how he knew of her, he ran a shaking hand through his wind-disheveled hair. Wide-eyed, he turned away, shook his head, then swung back to fix her with a frantic stare.

She was beginning to feel insulted.

"Citrine Sinclair?" he asked again. "One of the Sinclair Jewels?"

Mayhap he knew her father was a powerful laird and was only now regretting taking her? She crossed her arms in front of her chest to keep her gown on and shifted her weight to one hip.

"Aye!" she challenged him.

His breathing slowed as he continued to stare. Finally, he gave himself a little shake of the head, and his mouth opened. She felt a surge of vindication, knowing whatever he was about to say would be an apology.

She was wrong.

"*Shite.*"

CHAPTER 8

This was his betrothed!

Rory was no fool; he'd read the betrothal contract, then re-read it multiple times, looking for a way out.

Citrine Sinclair, one of the Sinclair Jewels and daughter to the powerful Laird Duncan Sinclair.

"Ye have sisters."

It was a stupid thing to say, but his tongue didn't seem to be working properly…not after that kiss and her revelation.

Her nod was hesitant, as if she couldn't understand his reaction. "Aye. Three of them."

What was wrong with him? Rory scrubbed a hand over his face, not sure how he should be reacting at all.

He'd *kidnapped* his own betrothed!

Part of him was ecstatic; all this time, he'd assumed his bride would be like his mother and sisters—biddable and demure. When he'd crossed swords with this firebrand —*Citrine*—for the first time, his heart and his cock had immediately wanted her, wanted to know more about her. She was *intriguing*.

And now she was *his*, even if she didn't realize it yet.

But another part of him was livid. His betrothed should've been sent to Lewes with all the pomp and ceremony demanded by the wedding of two powerful lairds' offspring. She'd been *barefoot*, by St. Ninian!

And her escort had allowed her to be taken by pirates.

The truth slammed into him with a clarity that had his gaze snapping back to her. "Ye were on yer way to Lewes, were ye no'?" Her ship had been heading for the Minch, and now she was heading eastward once more. "For yer wedding."

Her brows rose. "Ye ken of my betrothal?"

"Aye, I'm—" He bit down on the words, wondering how much to share with her.

No matter the current ridiculousness, if they *did* end up married, could he trust her to keep his secret? Could she live on Lewes while he was gone pirating and *not* reveal his identity?

But if they ended up married, she would recognize him as the Black Banner, no matter how much time had passed. Mayhap it would be better to confess all now?

Nay, because there was no guarantee this misadventure would end in a wedding, despite the contract. And if they went their separate ways, then her being ignorant of his identity was for the best.

And she was still standing there, waiting for his confession.

"I'm a MacLeod," he finished weakly.

She hummed and nodded, one hand holding up her gown at the shoulder. "'Twould explain yer claim that the pearl had been in yer family, I suppose."

It was his turn to blink in confusion and drop his hand instinctively to the pouch at his belt. "The pearl?"

Her chin jutted toward him in that adorable way he was coming to recognize as her being mulish. Or combative.

He liked it, and despite the circumstances, felt a smile tugging at his lips.

"Ye claimed the pearl belonged to yer family, but I *ken* it belongs to mine. It's been on Lewes all these years, has it no'? 'Twas the reason I agreed to this farce of a betroth—"

Her cheeks flushed, and she dropped her gaze as she bit off whatever she had been saying.

Farce of a betrothal?

Was it possible she felt the *same exact way* about this contract?

She was obviously trying to change the subject when she peeked up at him again. "Do ye... Do ye ken my betrothed? Rory, son of the laird?"

He was tempted to reply with a witticism about his own handsomeness or prowess with the ladies, but the words stuck in his throat. The instinct to impress her warred with the need to end the contract and ensure neither would have to be married.

So, he shrugged weakly. "The island isnae that large."

She nodded, inferring what he wanted her to, that he knew her betrothed but not well.

By His Blood, this was a complication he'd never considered when he'd crossed swords with her.

"Come," he said gruffly, blowing out a breath. "Let us return."

If the birlinn hadn't been completely beached yet, mayhap they could get a few miles closer to Sinclair lands. As much as he hated the idea of saying goodbye to her, it would be for the best to send her back home.

But would she stay there? Or would her father put her on another ship and send her back to Lewes? Were there other pirates who would attack her?

Rory's hands curled into fists as his blood began to heat, thinking of her in danger once more.

She was his *betrothed*, by St. Ninian, and he'd kill any man who thought to harm her.

Nay, nay, he reminded himself. *She'd* kill any man who thought to harm her.

The thought forced his lips to curve wryly, and he blew out another breath, trying to calm his anger.

When he glanced her way, she was struggling to tie up her laces under her arm. He stepped up beside her, brushed her hands out of the way, and made short work of helping her lace her gown.

It was a shame to watch all that glorious, golden skin disappear under the green silk, but she was *his*, and he'd not allow any other man—not even his friends and crew—to ogle her.

When he finished, she slanted him a glance under her lashes that made his cock—which had been doused in icy reality upon learning her name—jump once more.

"Thank ye," she whispered huskily.

He shrugged. "Well, I prefer to *unlace* women, but I suppose—"

Clot-heid! He shook his head. *Ye're no' supposed to brag of yer exploits to yer betrothed!*

But she didn't know she was his betrothed, did she? *Bah!* This was going to be difficult to navigate.

She was the one who bent to retrieve the leather bag with the box inside and began to move around the outcropping of rock toward where they'd left the boat. When she peeked back over her shoulder at him, Rory jumped into motion.

He was surprised how far they'd walked. But remembering her taking his hand and leading him away from his crew only a short time ago, he also recalled enjoying the way she took command. And truthfully, he'd been admiring the way the gown swung about her backside and legs.

Now, though, he caught up with her easily, and they

walked in silence for a few moments before he cleared his throat. "We've been heading toward Durness. I was going to leave ye there, thinking ye could make it home from there. But if ye'd like…" When had he gotten so noble? "We'll take ye to Reay, among yer kinsmen."

She slanted a glance his way. "Thank ye," she said quietly, her grip white-knuckled on the bag. "I'll…" She shook her head and blew out a breath, as if confused. "I suppose I'll return home and tell my father of William's betrayal. And then…" She shrugged. "I intended to head to Lewes, if only to retrieve that pearl ye hold." She halted and whirled on him suddenly. "I dinnae suppose—Nay, never mind."

He stopped as well, brows raised. "What?"

"I cannae imagine ye have much access to the MacLeod's keep on Lewes and the jewels I seek would likely be held by the family."

Jewels? Rory was having trouble following what she meant. "Ye and yer sisters…ye're named for jewels, aye?"

Nodding, she held the bag against her chest. "Agata and Saffy are married to powerful lairds"—she said this with a glare, as if it would influence him—"and Pearl is happy living with her husband in the village outside my father's keep."

Pearl. *Pearl.* Rory's eyes widened as he reached into his pouch for the pearl he'd always carried, as he nodded to the bag in her arms. "Agate. Sapphire." He lifted his stone, rolling it across his knuckles. "*Pearl.*"

Taking a deep breath, she nodded again. "They are the Sinclair jewels, Banner. Stolen generations ago from my family. My sisters and I…we've been working together to find them. When Da betrothed me to the MacLeod lad, I thought 'twould be my opportunity to find the remaining two. But then…"

"But then ye were attacked by pirates," Rory finished

thoughtfully, staring at the bag she held and trying to ignore the "lad" description.

"Aye, and it turned out one held my family's jewel."

Her family's jewel? He almost scoffed aloud. Surely, she realized this cold pearl in his hand *wasn't* the jewel her father loved most in the world? Not when he had Citrine for a daughter and presumably three others just as valuable?

She was the treasure.

But then she tossed her head, and the hair she hadn't seemed able to control flopped back over her shoulder. "Look, I'll show ye."

To his surprise, she dropped to her knees there in the sand and tugged the box from the bag. Smoothing out the leather, she placed the bag on the ground, then reverently opened the box.

She pushed the pouches containing the jewels out of the way and reached for the material underneath. As Rory crouched beside her, he was surprised to see her unfold a tapestry, old and faded. Draping it over the bag to keep it out of the sand, she smoothed her palm over the ancient fibers.

"See?" she whispered, pointing to the circle in the center. "This is the Sinclair brooch, the symbol of my family's power." The circle was green with four circles within it. "The brooch is made of malachite." She pointed to the circles in turn. "Agate, sapphire, pearl, and citrine."

Rory cocked his head as he studied the rendering before him. The agate and sapphire in the box certainly looked as if they matched the stones portrayed in the tapestry.

Reaching slowly, he held the pearl above the picture…then placed it gently on the place of the pearl in the tapestry.

The image was slightly larger, but it was no doubt the pearl he'd always carried had once belonged on a brooch. Likely this one.

He lifted his gaze to meet hers and saw no hostility there.

Just certainty. She was *certain* he would see the truth in her claim…and he had.

"Why would a pearl from the Sinclair brooch be on Lewes with the MacLeods?"

She shrugged. "I dinnae ken. But they've been split up." She pointed to the thick design encircling the brooch in the tapestry. "Ye see here? It says 'Mackenzie', which was convenient, because Agata was on her way to marry the laird's regent. Once there, she found the agate and evidence another stone was with the Sutherlands—"

"Wait," he interrupted. "What evidence?"

"How much time do ye have?"

It was said in such a wry tone, Rory didn't bother to hide the chuckle which escaped his lips. To prove he was interested, he moved his leg and plopped to his arse beside her. The tall cliffs rose on one side, and the crashing ocean on the other made it necessary to raise their voices. But when he glanced down the beach toward his men, he could see Bull had them well organized.

Rory could afford to sit here with his betrothed a while longer.

And Citrine did the same, shifting so her knees were in front of her and her bare feet planted in the sand. As she wrapped her arms around her knees, her skirt pulled up, and he could see her toes digging into the granules.

As he was still barefoot, too, he did the same, and as always, the sensation soothed him.

"Agata is a painter, ye see." Citrine took a deep breath, held it, then released it. "When she saw the Mackenzies' wooden map, she jumped at the chance to examine it. I dinnae ken the entire story, but it had something to do with a saying Jaimie— that's her new husband—Jaimie's aunt used." She shrugged. "It led her and Jaimie—and her stepson, wee Callan—to discover the sapphire within the map, under the Sutherland holding."

A jewel *in* a map? Rory whistled softly. "Sounds like an adventure."

She nodded, her attention on the tapestry. One long finger traced the image of the deep, blue sapphire, and Rory was struck by the realization this woman likely would never sit quietly and embroider while her husband went a-pirating.

He wasn't sure if that was a good thing or not.

"I wanted to go to the Sutherlands. Our youngest sister, wee Pearl, was engaged to the Sutherland Devil, ye ken," she said quietly, her attention still on the tapestry. "Years ago, he tried to kill the man who is now her husband."

"Really?"

She glanced up at him and gave a quick jerk of her chin. "Merrick Sutherland is a hard man who administers swift justice, but…" She shrugged, her lips twitching as she looked back down at the tapestry. "I like him. Saffy does, too. I couldnae leave home because—well, I couldnae leave our father. Saffy is nae a warrior, but she accepted the mission to infiltrate the Sutherland holding and did it as a lad."

The mission to infiltrate the holding…

She sounded like one of his men, and the comparison made him smile. "She was dressed as a lad, ye mean?"

"She became the Sutherland's squire, and together they defeated a threat to his rule. They *also* found my clan's sapphire, behind a stone in the dungeon. A stone with the MacLeod of Lewes' crest carved into it."

Rory rested his weight on a palm and frowned slightly as he considered the implications.

"'Tis why ye accepted this *farce of a betrothal,* aye? To follow the trail of clues to Lewes?"

"Aye! There'd be nae other reason to chain myself to a lad so far from home."

A lad? There was that assumption again.

He cocked his head. "Rory MacLeod might be the youngest

of his father's children, but he's nae a lad." Before she could accuse him of knowing the man, he latched onto her other words. "And plenty of women accept husbands who live far from their homes."

"They're no' me!" She was angry, he could tell. But despite her emotions, she was careful when she lifted the tapestry and folded it to place back in the box. "My clan—my *father*—needs me. He's in danger, and I wouldnae have left him had it no' been vital to our future!"

That's right...he squinted over her shoulder, trying to remember. "Is there no' a legend tying the brooch to yer clan? My grandmother's stories—"

He didn't complete the thought, knowing it might identify him as being of the laird's blood. But she didn't seem to notice. She was carefully placing the tapestry away, having moved the pearl out of the way.

"Aye. 'Tis said that the Sinclair's power rests in the brooch. Without it, we are doomed to die and fade into obscurity. Already two of my sisters have accepted names and homes away from the Sinclairs. My sister Pearl is married to my father's bodyguard, the Sinclair Hound. At least she's home with him."

She took a deep breath and looked up, meeting Rory's gaze with a fierceness in her own. "I'm sorry to betray yer kinsman, Banner, but I'll no' marry a MacLeod and rot away on Lewes. I plan on finding the rest of the jewels and returning them to the Sinclairs. Then I'll stand beside my father and ensure our clan does *no'* fall to stupid superstition."

The pride and certainty in her voice was enough to make him smile. Enough to make him want to cheer her on.

But was it enough to give her his pearl?

He hummed slightly as he reached for it, rolling it across his knuckles, then dropping it to land heavy and familiar in his palm. He remembered finding it. He remembered how he'd always wondered what it meant and why it didn't feel completely his.

"How did ye come to own that?" she asked quietly.

Could he tell her without revealing his identity? If there was one thing he was certain of, it was that he didn't want to lie again to this woman. This woman who was his betrothed and had no intention of honoring the contract with her name on it.

"I…found it," he began hesitantly. "When I was a lad in the MacLeod keep. I was playing—well, it matters no'. 'Twas hidden in a carved design in a bed."

"A *bed*?" Her brows went up.

"It was…in the lady's chambers."

There. Mayhap she'd wonder why a lad who grew up to be a pirate might be wandering through the chambers of the laird's wife, but it could be explained if he were the son of a servant.

She apparently wasn't thinking of it, though. Instead, she hummed as she placed the pouches with the agate and sapphire back into the box.

"Just like the Mackenzie map. She must've commissioned someone to carve a compartment," Citrine murmured.

"She?" Unconsciously, Rory rolled the flat-sided pearl across his knuckles and back again.

Taking a deep breath, Citrine closed the box, slid it into the pouch, and met his eyes.

"Three generations ago, four Campbell sisters married Highland lairds. Sutherland, Mackenzie, Sinclair, and…" The fingers of her other hand shook just briefly before she touched her fingertips to his shin. "MacLeod."

Anything he might've said had been completely forgotten at the sensation of her touch. He fought the urge to shudder as warmth spread up his leg to his groin.

"We dinnae ken why they chose to split up the brooch, but

my theory is the one who married my great-grandda—his second wife—sent the stones to her sisters."

The stones. Rory swallowed. "Ye've found two of the four now?"

"Nay." As she shook her head, the hand which had touched him moved toward the pearl in his hand. Instead of taking it, however, she closed his fingers around it. "*Three* of the four. I just pray there wasn't a *fifth* Campbell sister holding the last jewel."

"The citrine," he whispered.

Her eyes flashed with golden fire when she nodded in determination. "I *will* find it, Banner."

The pearl was growing heavier in his hand, so Rory tucked it back in its pouch. He wasn't ready to part with it yet.

If he gave it to her, he'd have no excuse to continue by her side, would he?

His mind made up, he rolled to his feet, hearing her gasp of surprise.

Standing there, toes digging into the sand and rocks, dressed in only his black plaid, he knew he wanted to continue with her. It was his pearl, was it not? His family was involved in her quest, her mission.

And after all, she *was* his betrothed, even if she didn't realize it.

He held his hand out to her, and without hesitation, she placed hers in it. When he pulled her to her feet, he made sure not to tug too hard. She rose beside him as if she belonged there and met his gaze as an equal.

"I apologize, Citrine Sinclair, for terrorizing ye so thoroughly. I took ye off yer ship and away from yer mission, thinking only of my own desires."

She didn't acknowledge his apology, but neither did she drop his hand. "And now?" she asked softly.

This decision had the potential to change not just his

career as the Black Banner and the livelihoods of his men…
but his future marriage.

He hesitated not a bit.

"I am no' ready to give ye the pearl, Citrine, but I hope ye'll
allow me to accompany ye on yer quest. My men and I will
ensure ye make it home safely."

Her eyes had gone wide with surprise. "Ye *are* honorable."

"Aye," he said with a smile. "And I'll even return yer sword."

She gave an unexpected snort. "Return my sword, find me
a pair of boots, trews, and a tunic, and I'll gladly accept yer
help!"

They were still holding hands when she scooped up the
bag and they began to walk down the beach toward his men.
And to Rory…it felt *right*.

Mayhap being betrothed wouldn't be so bad if this firebrand was to be his wife?

CHAPTER 9

CAMPING on the beach with pirates was terrifying.

And exhilarating.

Citrine couldn't recall laughing as much as she did that evening, and it was all thanks to the man by her side. The Black Banner—whatever his real name—was kind and went out of his way to make her laugh.

She had to assume it was because he found out who she really was and realized kidnapping the daughter of a Highland chief wasn't a good idea. He wanted to avoid her father's vengeance.

As if she ever told her father what happened....

Earlier, she'd been willing to bed this man like a common whore…and even now she had a few hours to think on it, she couldn't regret her decision. Despite the circumstances of their meeting, he made her feel…well, *good*.

"Well, lads," he called as they returned to the camp on the beach, "Lady Sinclair kens we're MacLeods, so dig out yer plaids afore some curious passerby decides to report the Black Banner's crew to the MacKay!"

To Citrine's surprise, that announcement was met with

cheers and laughter and more than a few men who dropped their trews or black kilts then and there. Determined not to show her discomfort, she just rolled her eyes toward the cliffs and kept them there until the teasing stopped.

"Ye can look now," came Banner's low voice near her shoulder. As always, it sent shivers down her spine in the most wonderful way. "Most of the lads are clothed again."

"*Most* of them?"

He chuckled. "Well, Bull and his men are still in the water, but 'tis cold enough their bollocks have likely climbed up inside them, so ye'll see naught untoward when they emerge."

With a groan at his poor joke, she turned on him, thinking to tell him she'd seen enough bare arses to last a year, *thankyeverramuch.*

But the words got caught in her throat when she saw what he was holding.

"'Tis the best we could do," he said sheepishly with a shrug. "Jock's trews should be long on ye, but with a bit of line as a belt, they'll do. The shirt's clean, at least."

Citrine's hands shook a bit as she took the clothing from his arms. The trews *were* a bit long, but Jock—the wiry one— was taller than her. They didn't smell the freshest, but they weren't as bad as some of the other clothing the crew wore. The white shirt was indeed clean and looked large enough to have been Banner's. And the tunic was made from the MacLeod tartan, but would fit her well.

She lifted it in question.

To her surprise, Banner shuffled his feet awkwardly. "Wee Ellis didnae mind sharing his best tunic with ye, if ye'll grant him one of yer gowns in exchange."

Keeping a serious face, Citrine nodded. "I hope he feels beautiful in it."

Banner snorted and knocked his shoulder against hers as if they were compatriots. "'Tis for his mother, ye clot-heid!"

She gave up trying to control her chuckles but told herself she was just laughing at the jest...not because being with him made her giddy.

Right.

After they got themselves under control, he led her to a crevice in the cliffs, then held up a yellow and black plaid to grant her some privacy while she changed. She hurried, her gaze intent on the blanket.

He didn't once try to peek.

He really was an intriguing sort of pirate, wasn't he?

The shirt was far too large, but she rolled up the sleeves and liked the way it enveloped her. Had it not carried *his* scent, she might not feel that way, but just as waking up in his arms that morning had made her feel safe, so, too, did wrapping herself in his shirt. Besides, the smaller tunic would hold it—and her breasts—in place.

Emerging, she held up the trews with one hand and gestured grandly with the other. "How do I look?

Turning, he tossed the plaid over one shoulder and ran a gaze from her toes to her head. He placed a hand on his hips and pursed his lips, as if deep in thought.

"Hmm." He waved at her legs. "From the hips down, without shoes, ye look like a lad in sore need of a good meal, strong discipline, and a spot on a sea-going vessel."

She struggled to keep her grin under control. "And from the hips up?"

His gaze snapped to hers, and she gasped at the heat she saw in his eyes. "Ye look like a lass who verra much is in need of a good kiss."

Oh.

When he stepped toward her, she sucked in another fast breath, thinking he might make good on that promise. But he only reached for her waist, and the thin rope—which he called a line—Jock had provided. Banner made fast work of tying up the trews and showed her how to easily untie the knot.

"When ye're ready to re-tie it, try this one." His fingers seemed to pass *through* each other as he deftly wove the line into a knot.

She chuckled, realizing they were both staring at her waist. "I had nae idea there were so many knots. I'd like to learn more, but not in my trews."

Stepping back, he winked at her, his hands falling to his belt. "Fair enough. I'll teach ye tomorrow, on the way to Reay."

She meant to ask how far away they were, but at that moment, he unhooked his belt, and his kilt *fell off*.

A true lady probably would have squealed and turned around.

Citrine didn't, but in her defense, it was because he'd left her no time. One moment he was standing there in his black kilt, looking as magnificent as always, and the next…

He was looking even *more* magnificent.

Mayhap it was the way he was smirking. Mayhap it was the way his shoulders flexed when he propped one fist on his hip. Mayhap it was the way the muscles of his stomach seemed to form a sort of V which drew her gaze downward to…

Oh.

She knew what a cock was. She'd felt one before, aye, but the sight of this one made her knees weak and her stomach tighten.

Christ and all of his apostles could've walked ashore right then, and she wouldn't be able to drag her eyes away from his member nestled in a patch of dark brown hair, which was growing before her eyes.

Oh my.

"Whoops," he quipped, not at all repentant, as he turned around and grabbed for the plaid over his shoulder. He made short work of folding it properly and wrapping it around his waist, and Citrine was a little disappointed to see that fine arse disappearing under the MacLeod plaid.

Was it her imagination, or was he tanned *all over*?

Part of her was irritated at her inability to contain her lust. She was betrothed to this man's kinsman, and even if she wasn't, there was an important quest to fulfill! But another part of her scoffed at that reasoning, reminding her that the betrothal wasn't of her choice, and why *shouldn't* she enjoy the sight of a beautifully sculpted, male body?

The arguments swirled in her head, so she was scowling when he turned back. "Ye did that on purpose," she accused.

And Banner, damn him, merely shrugged. "Aye, mayhap. I wanted to see if ye'd be as embarrassed as ye were earlier."

She glared at him. "Go find me my sword, Banner."

His laughter burst out of him and he gestured her back toward the camp and the ship. But he hadn't ignored her threat. "Come along, Lady Sinclair. Ye can have a second go at me."

To her surprise, not only was Banner an expert swordsman, but a better-than-average teacher. It turned out that Bartholomew had rescued her sword—"I was going to give it to Char—to the Black Banner's niece, but he says ye should have it back."—and handed it to her with good grace.

She felt so much more at ease with her sword in her hand and those ungainly skirts out of the way, despite being barefoot in the rocky sand.

Banner was the one to initiate the sparring, dividing his men—the ones who weren't working—into pairs. He paired off with her, and although she could tell he wasn't putting his full strength into the blows, she appreciated that they were both working up a sweat.

Although she refrained from showing him everything she knew, he taught her a few new moves, including a leap she'd never seen before. Not only was he patient with her, he was willing to repeat the same series of moves over and over again without complaining, until she felt confident she could remember everything.

He was the one to call a halt to the sparring, raising his hand with a grin, then flashing his gaze around the other men. As she sheathed her sword and moved up beside him, he began calling out corrections to the pairs of men spread around the beach. She could see where he got his practice in teaching.

He really *was* a leader.

It was a shame he wasted his talents as a pirate. She could imagine him as a laird in a Highland keep, commanding respect and devotion. He'd lead his men into the future with a fair and balanced mind, as well as a firm grip on his sword. All he lacked was a strong woman by his side—

Whoa there, lass! She shook her head. *Stop daydreaming. Ye dinnae even ken if he's married!*

Well, that was easy to remedy.

"Ye're verra good at this," she blurted. "Yer wife must be proud."

He twisted toward her so quickly, he might've hurt his neck, but his expression was one of surprise.

"I'm no' married," he said.

"Ye're no'?" She'd been willing to bed him, and was only now considering this problem?

He shook his head, then took a deep breath. "I am betrothed, but 'tis…complicated."

In many places, a betrothal was as good as a marriage. But the Blessed Virgin knew Citrine didn't think of it that way. Mayhap Banner didn't either.

He stepped back a bit as he reached once more for his sword. "Would ye like another go?"

She grinned. Her body might be urging her to grapple in bed with him, but she *always* enjoyed a good sparring.

After, she would've liked to bathe in the surf, the way more than a few of Banner's men were doing. But she contented herself with wading out and splashing water on her face and the nape of her neck. Someone had found her a leather tie for her hair, and she appreciated it.

It turned out that one of Bartholomew's hunting parties had been successful, and the older man roasted the hares which had been taken down by wee Ellis's sling. Citrine sat cross-legged in the sand beside Banner and enjoyed the flavorful meat and jokes the men traded.

She was in a remote place, surrounded by pirates. She *should* have been worried, but with her sword on her hip and Banner at her side, she wasn't. It remained an odd realization.

"Ye did well today, Citrine." He nudged her with his shoulder. "Ye're used to training?"

"Aye. Da didnae approve at first, but I was young and wore him down. I try to train daily, but sometimes other duties—as the laird's daughter—come first. William was my partner, usually."

He hummed as he chewed, then very carefully didn't look at her when he nonchalantly asked, "William? He's the coward who stood aside to let a fierce pirate take ye?"

The meat turned ashy in her mouth, but she forced herself to swallow and lowered the bone she was pulling the meat from. "Aye," she said in a quiet voice, staring at the fire. "I thought… We *used* to be friends. But over the last years, I suppose he thought it was too awkward to spar with me?" Shrugging, she tried to pretend naught was amiss. "Dougal assured my father he'd be enough to protect me on my journey, but I cannae forget the way William just stood there."

"He's a coward." Banner's condemnation came fast and certain.

She shrugged again. "I didnae think so, but 'tis the only

explanation. But…he seemed almost *amused* that I was being kidnapped, and I didnae think he'd be so petty."

Thankfully, Banner didn't ask more about the history between them, although she wasn't sure why it should matter. Her past was her own business, and Banner wouldn't care one way or the other. It wasn't as if there was a future between them, not when they were each betrothed to other people.

Instead, he asked an unexpected question. "Who is Dougal?"

She glanced at him, at the way the fire reflected in his eyes and caused funny shadows across his cheeks when he smiled. He was genuinely interested in her life.

Citrine wanted to tell him.

She was used to being the strong one. The one her sisters relied on to have a plan and know how to implement it. Since her sisters' marriages, she missed that sense of place she'd once had among them. And she missed talking to them about the problems which plagued them all.

So, she took a deep breath and told Banner all about Dougal and how she'd come to trust him less in recent years. She told him about Da's sickness and how she suspected Dougal of poisoning him but couldn't prove it. She listened as Banner responded to her theories and offered some of his own.

Then, as the evening wore on and they both took pulls from the wineskin, she told him of her sisters' marriages and how lost she felt. In turn, he spoke of his own family, although he didn't tell her any names. Except…

The stars were out, and they were both lying on their backs, watching them twinkle above. The night had turned cold enough that she was pleased for his warmth beside her. He lay with one arm stacked behind his head, and somehow, her head had ended up on his shoulder.

"Ye remind me of my niece, Charlotte," he murmured. "She

and her twin brother, Tavish, are my auldest brother's youngest bairns. She's as wild and free as the north wind. Tav says he wants to be the Black Banner when he grows up."

"Will ye let him?" Happy he was sharing his history with her, she rolled slightly so she was facing him, her cheek still pillowed on his shoulder. "When ye retire?"

"Retire?" He hummed derisively, his eyes still focused on the stars. "At sea, I'm in control. On land, I'm merely another son—I mean…" He blew out a breath, and she saw his eyes dart in her direction. "I have nae place except at sea. Here, I'm the *Black Banner*. My men will go through the fires of hell for me. How could I give that up?"

Not for the first time, Citrine realized this man was no crofter, no peasant. Who was he? A younger son, he'd said. Surely not a nobleman—none of them would allow their sons to become pirates. But mayhap a merchant's son? Someone who might expect to become a captain?

But he wouldn't tell her, and she wouldn't ask.

Here and now, they were just two people without pasts and without futures.

Together.

As if he understood, his arm tightened around her. "Go to sleep, Citrine. Ye'll need all yer strength for the knots I promised to teach ye."

She was smiling when she gave into his suggestion and closed her eyes.

THE NEXT MORNING, they broke their fast with surprisingly good porridge Bull made, then Banner lifted her into the birlinn and stripped out of his plaid once more. This time she kept her attention on the horizon, even when she knew he'd clamored, wet and bare-arsed, back aboard.

She'd seen enough of his naked body yesterday to keep her company in her dreams.

Still, when he stepped up beside her on the aft deck, chuckling as he re-belted his plaid, she felt her lips twitch.

"Coward," he murmured.

"Tease," she shot back, and then they were both chuckling.

He was true to his word, teaching her how to tie various knots in between his other duties as they sailed eastward. To her surprise, the rest of his men joined in, calling out suggestions or tricks to make things easier. After knots, they moved on to jigs, and Auld Marcus pulled out his pipes for accompaniment.

She couldn't help comparing this voyage to the westward one with the merchant vessel and William. There, she'd been worried and bored. Now she had the third Sinclair jewel—or at least knew where it was—and was heading home to regroup. And she was having *fun*.

Afternoon found her sitting in the shade of the ship's side —Banner called it the gunwale—stitching the sail beside a talkative Bartholomew. She was teasing him about the size of his stitches, and the rest of the crew were taking turns making up verses to songs. The favorite seemed to be the one they'd sung the afternoon she was taken. So much had changed in such a short amount of time!

When the refrain started again, she joined in.

"One of brown, and one of white,
And one of the deepest blue!
One glows gold in the fire's light,
Jewels in the hearthstone's view!"

This time, however, it was Banner who indicated he'd be singing the next verse. He stood, legs spread, and bare feet planted on the deck, his shoulders tan in the sunshine and his smile near blinding.

His men cheered when he lifted one hand from the rudder and waved, then began in his deep, clear voice,

"She's fierce and bold and lovely,

With her sword she'll make her stand.

Her eyes flash gold in the sun's pure light,

She's my lady, my firebrand!"

All the verses evoked cheers, but this one seemed special. More than a few men leapt to their feet to pull off their tams and waved them in appreciation, even as they all—Citrine included—broke into the refrain.

"One of brown, and one of white,

And one of the deepest blue!

One glows gold in the fire's light—"

With a gasp, Citrine dropped her awl, unable to finish the refrain.

One glows gold in the fire's light.

A firebrand, he'd called her, for the color of her eyes.

She jumped to her feet in her excitement, her eyes finding Banner's across the deck.

He immediately stepped forward, keeping one hand on the rudder, concern on his face. "Lass? What is it?"

The song died around them, and Citrine realized she was clenching and unclenching her hands at her sides, a tingling spreading throughout her body.

This was *it.*

She wasn't sure how she knew, but she knew she—*they*—were close.

"The song," she whispered.

When he frowned, she realized he hadn't heard her. "The song," she repeated. "The refrain."

"Marcus! Come take over!" He called the command, then met her in the middle of the aft deck. He took her hands. "What about the song, Citrine?"

She pulled one hand out of his grip and laid her fingertip

on her right cheek, pointing at her own eye. "One glows gold in the fire's light."

By his little head shake, it was clear he didn't understand, and she struggled to make him. "My sisters all have the same hair color, but our eyes are different hues. Agata's are brown, Saffy's are dark blue, and Pearl's a blue so light, ye think it silver."

He still seemed confused when he nodded encouragingly. "Aye? 'Tis why yer mother named ye after the jewels in the—"

When he sucked in a breath, she knew he understood, and nodded in excitement. "One of brown and one of white. That's the agate and pearl."

"And one of deepest blue—the sapphire."

Smiling, they both said, "One glows gold in the fire's light," together, but he was the one to lift his hand to her cheek. "*Citrine.*"

"Aye!" She nodded, careful not to dislodge his touch, which made her feel as if she had a partner in this. "The song—'tis a MacLeod song, aye?—is about the *jewels*! Mayhap the Campbell sister who traveled to the MacLeod clan was the one who made up the song in the first place?"

"But why?" Banner dropped his hand and shook his head. "What would be the purpose?"

She was the one to grab his hand this time. "To tell us where the last stone is! *Jewels in the hearthstone's view*! Do ye no' see? She's telling us where the citrine is!"

"In the hearthstone's view? Which hearthstone?"

Citrine felt like bouncing, or spinning, or at the very least, allowing her joy and laughter to bubble out in excitement. "The only one that matters! The jewel's hearthstone is in the Sinclair's holding, and I ken exactly which hearth it must be!"

He snaked his arm around her back, drawing her tight against him. His smile was bright when he looked down at her. "I think ye may be right, my wee firebrand."

She poked him in the chest but didn't bother hiding her answering grin. "No' so *wee*, Black Banner."

"Nor me." When he thrust his pelvis forward and waggled his brows lewdly, she felt his hardness and knew he was excited as well, but mayhap for a different reason.

Rolling her eyes at his crude joke, she nevertheless finally allowed her laughter free rein.

For the first time, she had a direction. Now she *had* to return home. There was every likelihood the citrine—the last of the Sinclair jewels—was hidden in the hearth of the very room she and her sisters had grown up in. It had belonged to the lady of the keep up until a generation ago, and it would make sense that the long-ago Lady Sinclair had hidden the last jewel right there in her very chamber.

Jewels in the hearthstone's view.

And now she had a plan to find the last of the missing jewels, present them to her father, and make a future for her people. A plan…and a partner.

Unable to contain her excitement, she wrapped her arms around Banner's neck and tugged him down to her lips. And when she kissed him, the crew erupted in cheers.

CHAPTER 10

RORY HADN'T EXPECTED to be saying goodbye to his crew, but when they reached Reay—as honest merchants, of course—he realized something important.

There was no way in heaven or hell he'd be saying goodbye to Citrine.

She was *his*, and he'd promised to help her on this mission.

Which meant he'd be accompanying her home.

So, he put Bull in charge of the birlinn, told Bartholomew to scrounge up some honest shipping work for them for a fortnight or so, and not to stray far from Sinclair lands. Rory could send for them if needed, and meanwhile…

Meanwhile, *he* would be with Citrine.

The two of them, plus the rest of the crew, spent another night in Reay so they could leave early. She didn't seem to mind the bawdy spirits around the campfire, and it had been her suggestion to stay on the beach with them.

So she wouldn't be recognized in town—that was her reasoning.

Personally, Rory hoped it was because she liked sleeping in his arms as much as he liked having her there. But after that kiss she'd given him on the birlinn, the result of her joy when she'd figured out the last clue…well, Rory went to sleep with a tented kilt again that night.

The next morning, she'd held his hand as he bid farewell to his men, and that sensation made him feel as if he could face anything.

Using some of their stolen coin, he purchased two horses from an ostler and liked the way her eyes lit up at the prospect of a quick return. He'd always preferred sailing to riding, but he discovered that with her beside him, the day passed easily.

Citrine was…

She was the salty north wind. She was a sturdy deck beneath his feet and the sound of taut rigging in the breeze. She was the feel of a good sword in his hand and the taste of a good ale on his tongue. She was funny and free and the most interesting woman he'd ever met.

How had he ever gotten so lucky when his father had signed that betrothal agreement? She was likely the only woman in the Highlands who could be this perfect for him.

And she still didn't know who he was.

The thought weighed on him. His reasonings for not telling her his identity, after discovering hers, were wearing away. Aye, if they parted at the end of this adventure, if they broke their contract, then her knowing his identity could be dangerous.

But as each hour passed in her company, Rory became more and more certain he wouldn't be parting with her.

Ever.

In fact, it was becoming increasingly difficult not to be touching her right now. Each time he looked her way, each time the wind caught her unruly blonde hair, each time her eyes sparkled in the sunlight, each time she chewed on her lower lip in thought, Rory's cock jumped.

The two kisses they'd shared had only left him hungry for

more, and as the afternoon wore on, he became determined to collect.

Finally, she pulled up on her reins. "I recognize this." She pointed to a crag in the distance. "The keep is beyond those cliffs. I've accompanied father's patrols this far out."

He sent her a quick grin. "Why am I no' surprised ye patrolled with the warriors?"

Shrugging, she swung down from her horse and led the animal to a wee burn meandering through the rocks. "I wanted to understand the lay of the Sinclair land. I've also visited as many of the crofters as I could manage within a day's journey."

Not for the first time, Rory recognized her competence. "Ye ken," he began, leading his own animal to the water. "Ye'd make a fine laird someday."

The look she cut him was part bitter, part resigned. "Aye, I ken it well. I've spent my life working for this clan, and I would make a fine leader." She took a deep breath and arched her back as she exhaled, stretching her aching muscles. "But as Dougal is fond of saying, a lass cannae be laird."

He hummed as he sank onto one of the large, mossy boulders. "And what does yer father say?"

Shrugging, she straightened and patted her horse's shoulder. "If he thought me worthy, surely he would've said so," she admitted in a quiet voice. "Instead, he withers away, thinking the clan is doomed to disappear without sons."

Two days before, she'd told him all about her clan's history with the missing brooch, and Rory agreed it was silly to pin all your hopes on a piece of jewelry. But if returning the jewels meant Duncan Sinclair recovered, it was a good enough reason for him to help.

Speaking of which…

"'Tis too late to continue on tonight, unless ye want to arrive home after dark?"

He didn't bother hiding the hopeful tone in his voice. He knew she'd be anxious to get home, but the thought of getting to spend another night in her arms...

To his relief, she sauntered over. "'Twould be rude to arrive so late," she said in a husky voice, promise in her eyes.

Thrusting himself to his feet, he found himself nodding. "Aye, *rude*. 'Twould be better to sleep and arrive in the morning."

She reached him, stopping just short of allowing her breasts to touch his chest. "*Sleep?*'

God's Wounds.

Rory's cock jumped to attention beneath his plaid, and he grinned. "Well," he drawled as he snaked an arm around her waist. "There *is* a little matter I've been meaning to take up with ye?"

"Oh, aye?" Her tone was innocent, but the mischievous look in her eyes anything but as she laced her arms around his neck.

"Aye," he growled. "About yesterday, on board the birlinn. Ye kissed me the way a woman kisses when she wants a man, kenning full well there was aught I could do about it in front of my men like that."

Her gaze focused on his lips. "That sounds harsh."

With a grunt of agreement, he pressed his pelvis forward, so she could see just how *hard* he was. "I have a mind to punish ye."

She shivered. "Punish? What do ye have in mind, Banner?"

Even the reminder she didn't know his name couldn't cool his ardor, but it *did* halt his playing. He lowered his lips to hers, and yet again marveled at her uninhibited reaction. She came alive in his arms, and he drank in her energy like a starving man.

She was the one who reached up and yanked at the ties holding the tunic and his old shirt closed, and he needed no further invitation. His lips left a hot trail across her skin, and he spent a moment marking her at the base of her neck.

Mine! the mark seemed to say. *She's mine!*

Even if she didn't know it.

Pushing aside the annoying feeling of guilt which was trying to worm its way into his enjoyment, Rory doubled his efforts to bring her pleasure. When his palm closed around her bare breast, and she moaned and arched against him, his body tightened in response. And the noise she made when he fastened his lips around that nipple...?

Well, it'd been a long time since he'd come undone against the inside of his kilt, and he wasn't going to start now.

Instead, he pushed her back against the boulder, waiting until she was able to support herself with outstretched arms. Then he sunk to his knees in front of her, ignoring her wordless cry of confusion as their lips parted.

They'd bought her new boots in Reay, but now he cursed the forethought as he struggled with them. As soon as he pulled them free, he turned his attention to the line she was using for a belt, and when he untied the knot, her trews sagged down.

Fortunately, she understood what he was about, and seemed to support it, judging from how fast she wriggled them down around her legs. Ellis's tunic molded to her, aye, but the white shirt she wore fell nearly to her knees.

Kneeling in front of her, Rory took a moment just to breathe, to try to get his erection under control. He remembered when he'd first lowered that plaid and seen her wearing his shirt... *beautiful.* Knowing the linen he'd once worn now caressed her skin was as close to holding her as possible.

But *now...*

With a devilish smile, Rory reached for her knees, pushing them apart. Her bare arse rubbed against the boulder as she repositioned herself, but when he reached for her thighs, she let her head fall back with a moan of desire.

When he reached the apex of her thighs and saw the dampness glistening in her curls, he knew she wanted him as much as he *needed* her.

He inhaled her scent, feeling like a man worshiping at a temple.

The first pass of his tongue across her slit had her gasping, but when his lips found the nub of her pleasure, she began to pray.

"Oh, Blessed Virgin!"

He smiled against her, reveling in the taste of her and knowing she was *his*.

Parting her folds, he slid one finger, then two inside her entrance, and her bottom lifted off the boulder, pressing closer to him.

The heel of her hand came to rest right where she wanted the pressure, her fingers playing with his hair as he licked and suckled at the core of her pleasure.

"Banner!" she panted, thrusting toward him once more.

She tightened around his fingers, and he mimicked the motion of his tongue, wondering if she could tell how much he'd rather be doing this with his cock. But by St. Ninian, he'd ensure her pleasure before he worried about his own.

"Banner!" Everything from her hold on him to her sheath tightened. Then he felt her pulsing around his fingers and smiled as he gently slid his tongue along her slit once more.

Spent, she collapsed. *"Goodness,"* she whispered, her breaths coming in gasps.

Smiling wider now, he pushed himself to one foot, then the other, gathering her in his arms as he rested with her against the boulder. It wasn't the most comfortable of spots, but he knew he'd never forget it.

He placed a kiss on her temple as she continued to pant. As

her breathing finally slowed, she grasped his forearm, leaning against his chest. "Banner. That was…" She shook her head.

"Do ye ken ye pray when ye find release?" he teased her. "Ye called on any number of saintly helpers."

"Aye, well…" She took two more breaths. "That was near heaven."

There in the cooling air of the late afternoon, he held his betrothed and laughed.

It was the horses who alerted them something was wrong. First one, then the other lifted their noses to the air, and Rory cursed his distraction. He was untangling himself from Citrine and reaching for his sword when the man stepped around a pile of boulders on the far side of the clearing.

Even without Citrine's gasp, Rory would've recognized him.

"William," she hissed.

Rory pushed away from the boulder, yanking his sword from its scabbard, and placing himself between the interloper and the woman he was coming to care for.

"What are ye doing here?" he growled in warning.

William didn't answer and made no move to halt. Instead, he sauntered closer, his eyes greedily raking Citrine's bare legs behind Rory. Despite knowing his shirt covered her thighs, Rory still felt the anger rising in his chest at the thought of this man's eyes on her.

And then the bastard spoke.

"I always kenned ye were a whore, Citrine," William lazily drawled. "Spreading yer legs for any—"

When he heard the sound she made—part sob, part denial —Rory stepped forward and thrust his blade at the other man. "How did ye return so quickly?"

William's hand was on his sword, but he shrugged noncha-lantly. "When Captain Angus finally returned to shore, I stole a horse and returned here as quick as I could. Ye ken…" He smirked. "To tell Dougal about the pirate who dragged Lady Sinclair off the ship to rape and murder her."

Behind Rory, he heard her suck in a breath, but he moved to place himself in front of her once more, so she wouldn't have to look upon this coward.

"Ye're scum and an affront to the Sinclair name. Yer commander will hear of this." It was an empty threat, as there's no way Dougal would believe Rory over one of his soldiers.

But William just shrugged. "Who do ye think told me to lose her on the way to Lewes?" He snorted. "Lose! Lewes! Ha!"

Lose her?

Red began to creep in at the edges of his vision when he realized what William was saying. "Ye *bastard*. Ye stood aside to let her be taken by pirates!"

"Aye!" William jerked his chin toward her. "And look at what the whore did! Spread her legs for ye willingly. Ye did no' even need to worry about raping—"

With a roar, Rory sprang for the other man, who managed to whip his sword out and up in time to block the blow. But Rory wasn't about to let that slow him down. He changed direction and attacked from a different angle, forcing the younger man to retreat.

"Dougal *wanted* Citrine taken? Why?"

William sneered as he blocked another attack. "She's the biggest threat to his lairdship." He brought his blade up, breathing heavily already. "If ye hadn't attacked the ship, I was to arrange another reason for her to disappear, then return home to report."

Arrange for her to disappear.

Rory's mind raced, jumping to a story Citrine had told him around the campfire of her younger sister's courtship. William had been part of the band escorting Pearl to the nunnery, and after Gregor whisked her to safety, the young man was the only survivor.

Citrine had pushed herself away from the boulder, but he was glad she hadn't yet reached for her sword. At her gasp, he knew she was thinking the same thing. He glanced her way, and nearly missed William's next attack.

But he had the upper hand soon enough and pushed the younger man back. "The attack on Pearl, ye bastard? Did ye arrange that, too? Were ye even wounded?"

Shrugging, William backed off, the tip of his blade beginning to falter. "Dougal said it was for the best if all the Jewels went missing. If he couldnae marry any of them—and Duncan had turned him down each time he'd suggested it—then it'd be better for them to die." He sucked in a few deep breaths as Rory's grip tightened on the hilt of his sword. "He was the one who told Duncan I'd been wounded."

Rory was tempted to use the sword to rip the plaid from the man's chest, to see if he really did bare the arrow scars Citrine said he'd claimed.

Exchanging a glance with her, seeing the fury in her eyes, he knew he'd content himself with planting his blade in the coward's chest.

Slowly, deliberately, he advanced on William, making sure the other man saw every drop of disgust he felt. "Ye're a coward and a traitor, and when ye die, nae one will mourn ye."

William's blade shook slightly as he lifted it, but the bravado in his voice was weak. "Ye're wrong. When Dougal is laird—and it willnae be long, once I kill Citrine and he finishes off Duncan—he's promised to make me his commander."

Dougal was the laird's cousin and might have a claim to the lairdship, but murder would never be honorable. And William had sealed his fate with his casual comment about harming Citrine.

With a wordless growl, Rory threw himself at his opponent once more, and this time he didn't waste breath with conversation. He slashed and swung as William fell back, his parries getting weaker and weaker until at last, the strength of Rory's blows broke through his defenses.

Rory buried his sword in the coward's neck, and William was dead before he hit the ground.

He paused, breathing heavy, the tip of his blade pointed at the ground, trying to control his rage. But he shouldn't have worried.

Citrine stepped up beside him, her legs still bare, her trews dangling from one hand. When she met his gaze, he saw his own fury mirrored in those flashing, golden eyes.

"Leave him here to rot like the scum he is," she growled. "We're going home."

Home.

He lifted his chin and inhaled, reveling in the lust which always coursed through his veins after a battle. But this time, it was shared with Citrine, and that was what made it valuable.

She grabbed his free hand and squeezed. "Get the horses. We're going into the keep to find the last jewel, but we'll do it tonight, without fanfare. If Da kens we're there, then Dougal will too. And now that we ken the full extent of his treachery—"

Cutting off the rest of her words, Citrine leaned forward and spat derisively on William's body. "Da willnae be safe until Dougal is forced to pay for his crimes."

Rory inhaled her scent, remembering her taste, and knew one thing for certain. "Ye'll no' face him alone."

She nodded, a grim smile on her lips. "Let's ride."

CHAPTER 11

GETTING into the keep shouldn't have been easy, but Citrine had spent years training with the men and knew the guard at the postern gate often slept. She was prepared to bribe him—or even subdue him, if it turned out he was loyal to Dougal—but he was true to his reputation and was snoring heavily as they snuck past him.

The kitchen entrance wasn't even guarded, although they startled Cook—a fat old man with only one eye—when they slipped inside. He was sitting at the table, a mug of ale in one hand and a piece of brown bread slathered in butter in the other, despite it being well after midnight.

Citrine halted so quickly, Banner's hand came to rest on her hip to keep from crashing into her. His touch reminded her of his *other* touch, the way he'd made her feel hours ago in the clearing. Before William had shown up and ruined—

Nay, better to not think of him and what they'd once shared. Better not to even think of Banner and the way he'd made her feel.

Best to focus on the mission at hand, which was in danger of being stopped if Cook sounded the alarm. What was he doing awake at this hour anyhow? They'd purposefully waited until the wee hours of the morning, sharing watch duties and napping in the shadows of the outer wall.

The older man shifted when he saw them and began to stand. But when Citrine stepped into the light of the candle, his one good eye widened in recognition. Slowly, he sank back down to the bench, switched his gaze to Banner—in his MacLeod plaid—and finally grunted in acceptance.

Lifting his mug of ale, he nodded to both of them, then took a sip.

Banner's hand on her hip gave a little squeeze, then released. She took that as a signal to continue, so she returned Cook's nod and exhaled softly, easing around the table.

But just as they reached the great hall, he stopped her with a hand on her hip again. She froze, one foot already on the top stair, and leaned back against him. His chest was warm against her back, and his breath tickled her hair when he leaned his chin over her shoulder to whisper in her ear.

"Men," he breathed. "On the benches."

She peered into the darkness, acknowledging he probably had the right of it. Despite her unorthodox ways, she'd rarely had reason to be in the great hall this late. Mayhap those *were* men sleeping along the walls…

After a long moment, she nodded to let him know she understood and eased her way into the space.

Neither of them made a sound as they crept across the rushes for the stairway.

Somewhere up there, God willing, her father slept safely. Was Dougal standing over him, a threat even in sleep? Now that Gregor was married, her father's most faithful bodyguard spent more time away from his laird.

Forcing down those thoughts, she made herself focus on the current situation. If they could find the last stone, she'd have something to give her father when she confronted him about the future and Dougal's very real threat.

As they crept up the stairs, her hands curled into fists, thinking about what William had said.

Dougal not only wanted to be laird next, he was willing to kill Duncan Sinclair to hurry things along. And although the threat to her life didn't bother her as much, Citrine was livid when she heard about William's part in the plot to harm Pearl. Those bandits could've *killed* her little sister, and would've, had Gregor not been there to save her!

Two good men died in that raid, and their deaths could be laid at William's feet as well. He'd arranged the attack, and had Pearl been killed, would've been the one to return home—likely grief-stricken—with the news.

In fact—as Citrine recalled it—he *had* returned before Pearl, and Dougal had been the one to tell Da all about William's bravely gotten wounds and Pearl's escape with Gregor.

Damn him to hell!

He *was* on his way to hell, Citrine was certain. The thought of what she'd once shared with him, the memory of his hands on her body, now made a sour taste in the back of her throat. Once, she'd thought him all she wanted in a man.

How much of what they'd done together influenced his actions? Was it possible he'd allied with Dougal because the promised commander position would offer him the power he used to joke about when he'd been bedding her?

He was ready to kill ye. He turned ye over to pirates!

She'd not allow herself to dwell on his motives or actions. He'd been a coward and a traitor, and now he was dead at the hand of one of those pirates.

And the Black Banner was a far better man than William had ever been.

Exhaling, she felt the tension in her shoulders lessen as

they reached the door to her chambers. She slipped inside and pulled Banner in after her, easing the door shut and pausing for sounds of pursuit.

When she heard nothing, she allowed herself to breathe again…right up until the moment he pulled her against him.

Her breasts were confined by the tunic, but she still felt her nipples tingle when they pressed against his chest. And when she hummed slightly in appreciation, she felt his member jump to awareness under his kilt and smiled in response.

"I need my wits about me, lass, and yet ye manage to drag my mind to my cock so simply?"

She chuckled, content in the knowledge no one would hear them. "Ye're the one who grabbed me!"

"I just wanted to ask ye where we were and why."

When she raised a brow, she knew he couldn't see her in the darkness. But he chuckled, and she felt it in her chest.

"Aright, fine. I *also* wanted to touch ye again."

So, she answered him honestly. "And I cannae wait for ye to touch me again. And I want to touch *ye*."

"But no' now." He sounded regretful as he pulled away, obviously taking a cue from her they no longer needed to whisper. "Is this where ye think the citrine is?"

She'd spent almost every night of her life here. It was easy enough to navigate in the darkness, and she knew right where the flint was kept.

"Aye," she said as she struck the spark to the candle wick. "'Tis the lady's chamber, but my mother never slept here. She died so long ago I hardly remember her, but she and Da had a love match, and she slept in the laird's bed with him."

When she held up the lit candle, she was sure the glow showed him not only her satisfied smile, but the excitement she was feeling.

"My sisters and I made this our room after we outgrew the

nursery. And when we were small, we explored every inch of the place."

"And what did ye find?"

Grabbing his hand, she tugged him toward the hearth. *"This!"* she said proudly as she shoved the candle toward the stone.

He crouched down and bent his neck, and she knew the moment he realized what he was looking at because he let out a low whistle. *"By His Wounds!"*

"Aye! See? My sisters and I even tried to chisel it out years ago, to see why it was special!"

In the back of the hearth, among the stones lining the chimney, there was a large one with an ornate eye carved into it. Pearl had always thought it creepy, but Citrine had been fascinated by it.

"Agata told us it was likely a remnant of the auld religion, a watchful spirit to protect us."

"Jewels in the hearthstone's view," he whispered thoughtfully.

She sent him an excited smile. "Aye! 'Tis an eye carved into the hearthstone! What else could it mean? The Campbell sister who married my great-grandda would've stayed in this chamber!"

He shifted his weight, reaching out to balance himself. "What did ye find when ye dug it out?"

She shrugged, going down to her knees in the empty hearth and dribbling some wax on the stones to allow her to hold the candle in place. By pushing her upper body into the hearth, she could reach the carved eye, and when he grabbed her hips to steady them—or at least, that's what she *assumed* he was doing—she could press her back against the upper stones and use both her hands to reach for the carved eye.

"Naught, see?" she grunted, trying to get her fingernails into the edges of the stone. "I chipped away the mortar—

Nurse gave me a slap for getting my gown so dirty—but its… too…heavy."

Slumping, she braced her palm against the sooty wall and ducked her head to see Banner. "See? The stone is huge."

"Ye said the sapphire was found behind a stone in the Sutherland dungeon? Carved with the MacLeod crest?"

"But it was much smaller." Using her hand, she showed him the size Saffy had described. "Easier to pull."

"Let me in there to try."

"Nay, 'tis filthy—" She cut off her words with a startled squeak when he slapped her bottom.

"Out of the way, woman! A little dirt never hurt a man!"

Chuckling, she backed out and saw him pull a dirk from his boot.

"For the mortar," he explained.

Nodding, she gestured for him to take her place and chuckled again at the noises he made as he squeezed himself into the hearth. As the sound of the blade chipping away at the mortar filled the chamber, she looked down at herself.

Although it was difficult to tell against the wool, the soot of the hearth—although it hadn't been used lately—was all over the front of her tunic. And Jock's trews, never pleasant-smelling to begin with, were filthy now. When she tried to brush off the dirt, she only smeared on more with her sooty hands, and eventually gave up in defeat.

With a grunt, Banner wrenched at the stone. Citrine's gaze dropped to his arse, sticking out of the hearth, barely covered by the yellow-and-black plaid. How easy would it be to reach down, flip up his kilt, and touch him?

In this position, she could stretch her hand between his legs and cup his bollocks. From the way he'd felt pressed against her earlier, she knew he wasn't a small man. Would his bollocks feel heavy in her palms? Or would she end up distracted by his member?

Likely, she told herself honestly, and the thought made her smile.

The memory of what he'd done for her earlier, how he'd made her feel, warmed her from the inside. A *fullness* settled between her thighs, and she shifted to relieve the ache. It had been hours since he'd kissed her *there*, and if William hadn't interrupted them, how would it have progressed?

Citrine didn't lie to herself; she wanted Banner. She wanted to *bed* him, to *fuck* him. But more than that…she wanted to *make love* to him, and the thought was perhaps the most disturbing of all.

This was more than lust.

Ye dinnae even ken his name.

He had an adventurous spirit to match hers. He was honorable and a fine leader of men. He made her laugh and was *kind*. Knowing all that, did she *have* to know his name to want to make love?

Ye're betrothed to another.

But not for long. She'd only agreed to the betrothal to search for the third jewel, and Banner had brought it to her. So, she'd be breaking the contract no matter how Da felt.

No matter how *Dougal* felt.

Mayhap one day, when this was all in the past and the Sinclairs' future was secure, she'd have the courage to visit Lewes. Mayhap she'd meet her betrothed, the youngest son of the MacLeod, and share a laugh with him over what might've been.

But if she *did* make the journey, she was honest enough with herself to admit it would be for the chance to have one last glimpse of the MacLeod pirate who was slowly stealing her heart.

He'd offered to help her fulfill her mission, but she had no doubt he'd be returning home when it was done.

But not before she convinced him to relinquish the pearl.

He'd been willing to trade the sapphire and agate for a kiss. Would he be amenable to a trade again? Citrine's sooty fingers trailed along the open neckline of her tunic, the touch—and thought—making her shiver with desire.

She'd bed him for her own pleasure, but mayhap he'd think it only because of the trade?

Her circular thoughts were interrupted when he made a noise of defeat and slapped the stone.

"Apologies, Citrine," he said as he wriggled backward from the hearth, blowing out a breath. "I cannae budge it, even without the mortar."

On his knees now, he reached for his kilt to clean the blade of his dirk, but she stopped him.

"Nay!" She took the dagger from him and wiped it on her trews, offering him a lopsided smile. "I'm already filthy. Let's keep yer plaid clean as long as possible."

He took the dirk back with a thankful nod. "Well, 'tis unlikely to stay clean long. I agree the coincidence of an eye carved into a hearthstone is too great. The last stone *must* be under there!" He blew out a breath. "Mayhap we need more tools? But then we risk alerting Dougal—"

"Wait," she said hoarsely, cutting him off with a hand on his forearm. "The eye…"

It was his words which had made her look at the carving in a different way.

"*The hearthstone's view,*" she breathed, pointing to the eye. "Look what the eye is *viewing.*"

Sucking in a breath, Banner dropped his weight forward, to his hands again, and bent closer. She joined him, and together they followed the line of sight of the carved eye.

It was looking to the side of the hearth and down. She scrambled for the stones at the base, and sure enough…one was loose.

"*By His Wounds,*" Banner whispered as she wiggled the stone from its careful placement.

It popped out easily enough, but Citrine paused, her heart pounding. She exchanged a glance with him and loved the way his grin spoke of his excitement.

Snatching up the candle, he edged it closer to the empty hole. "Is the citrine in there?"

Bless him, he was as excited as she was!

With a deep breath, she shoved her hand into the empty space beside the hearth, and her fingers closed around something wrapped in smooth leather.

But when she pulled it out, it was far too large to be the citrine. Her hand shook as she unwrapped the mysterious object right there on the hearthstones of her childhood chamber.

When the candlelight revealed their treasure, Banner whistled softly, and Citrine slowly straightened.

The Sinclair brooch.

It was bigger than her hand, the green malachite gleaming in the candlelight. Just like in the tapestry, there were four empty spaces for four large, flat-bottomed jewels. With shaking fingers, she touched each of the empty settings.

"Agate, pearl, sapphire, and…"

Banner's hand covered hers. "*Citrine.* The last jewel wasnae in there?"

With a sinking feeling, Citrine suddenly lunged for the empty hole, praying she'd find another smaller bundle containing the last stone.

Nay.

She slumped in defeat. "'Tisnae there."

His curse was muttered, but she knew it meant he was equally disappointed. Still, his tone was cheerful when he scooped up the brooch and offered it to her.

"Well, ye still found the brooch. 'Tis no' something yer

father *or* Dougal is expecting. With three jewels and the brooch, ye can still offer it to the Sinclair."

She shook her head, the lump in her throat not allowing her to speak. He was *right*; finding the missing brooch—and right here in her own chambers!—was akin to a miracle. But she'd been so focused on finding the citrine, the knowledge she'd have to continue her quest was like a kick to the gut.

Mayhap it was because it was *her* namesake.

I am the last of the Sinclair Jewels. The last one at home, the last one to protect Da. And the missing stone.

"Citrine," he whispered, still holding the brooch out to her. "Did it no' ever occur to ye that *ye* could be the next laird? Ye told me the legend says only the most skilled and bravest Sinclair warrior can return the jewels and restore the clan to power, aye?"

She met his gaze in confusion, but he continued.

"Well, ye've gathered all but one of the stones and now have the original brooch. *Ye* are the bravest and most skilled warrior, Citrine," he finished in a whisper.

Nay, she wanted to protest! Of the Sinclair warriors, there were plenty who were braver and stronger and more skilled than she; she should know after training with them!

But none besides Dougal have a blood claim as strong as yers.

And she'd be damned before she allowed him to claim the lairdship. The man lacked honor, no matter his skill.

"I'm a woman," she finally managed to say.

And Banner, bless him, merely shrugged. "'Tisnae so unbelievable that a strong, brave, skilled, and *honorable* woman could become laird of a clan."

Could she? Could she return the jewels to her father and demand the right to rule after him?

Could she *rule*?

Swallowing, she reached for the brooch. "I dinnae ken..."

To her surprise, his hand closed over hers. Gently, he

turned her palm up and placed the brooch in her hand, then covered it with his hand. "I do," he said intently, staring into her eyes. "I *ken* ye can do it, Citrine Sinclair. Ye're the clan's Jewel, and *will* do it."

His faith was humbling.

But then he smiled and broke the spell, pushing to his feet.

"But for now, I'd say we need some food afore we challenge Dougal for yer rightful place."

Her stomach chose that moment to remind her how long it'd been since their last meal—eaten yesterday at noon in the saddle. "And mayhap a change of clothes." She grimaced down at herself, then around the empty chamber. "I almost regret having Pearl remove all the…"

When she trailed off, he raised a brow at her, and she met his gaze with a smile.

"I ken where we can go."

CHAPTER 12

THE COOK WAS SNORING in his little nook behind the kitchen chimney when they snuck back out of the keep, but his presence still made Rory nervous. The older man hadn't reacted negatively when he'd recognized Citrine, but would anyone else?

Who here was loyal to Dougal?

Mayhap it was that thought which had him drawing his sword as they crept past the oblivious gatekeeper and ghosted along the wall. But Citrine didn't object, not even when he paused to carefully scan the village for signs of life.

It couldn't be more than an hour or two 'til dawn, but the night air was still crisp with unusual summer chill.

Finally, she laid a hand on his forearm and leaned close enough for her breasts to brush against his shoulder, severely distracting him.

"Make for the far side. The last row of cottages on the left. Pearl and Gregor live there."

Her scent was so distracting—and his cock so attentive— he had trouble focusing on what she was saying. Instead, he offered a nod and slipped around the wall to head for the center of the village and beyond.

There *were* some people awake—a mother with a crying bairn, the baker already at work, and two men still laughing outside the tavern—but Rory was able to avoid them. However, when they reached the last row of cottages and Citrine stepped into the road, he grabbed her wrist.

In the moonlight, he could see her scowl, so he leaned close to her ear.

"Careful, firebrand. Ye dinnae ken who is faithful to yer Da."

Her frown deepened. "Gregor is his Hound, his most loyal warrior."

"Aye," he breathed, "but what of the others in these homes?"

From the widening of her eyes, he knew she understood. She gave a sharp nod, then slipped from the shadows of one cottage to the next. It took a bit longer, but made Rory breathe easier, and soon enough, they stood outside Pearl's door.

He waited for her nod before he sheathed his sword and scratched at the door.

It was a long wait before he heard movement on the other side of the door—the occupants were obviously still abed when he'd woken them. As the latch lifted, Rory knew he couldn't risk Citrine's brother-in-law standing in the doorway, loudly asking who woke him.

So, Rory lowered his shoulder, slammed into the door, and pushed the man—Gregor—back into the small home. He had just enough time to glimpse a quaint room with a bed behind a screen—a startled woman sitting up under the coverlet—and a cooking area, before they slammed into the table.

The man didn't speak, but his fists were loud enough. One slammed into the side of Rory's head, causing him to see flashes of lights, but he blocked the second blow before it crushed his nose. The larger man was reaching for Rory's neck, likely to choke him to death, when Citrine finally slipped inside and shut the door.

"Hold, Gregor," she hissed, then repeated the command louder.

The man, clearly surprised by her presence, held up his hands, in surrender and backed toward the bed. The woman, with long, blonde hair to match Citrine's, scrambled out from the coverlet.

"Citrine?" Pearl cried, throwing herself toward her sister. "William told us ye'd been taken by pirates!"

The sisters embraced, not caring about the soot covering Citrine, and Rory's lips lifted at the obvious relief and joy in their hug.

Until he glanced at Gregor and saw the man's scowling eyes flick between Rory and the door.

Rory shrugged and lifted his hands in surrender. "Sorry. Couldnae risk ye making any noise and alerting passersby before we ken who to trust."

The man's expression eased, and in the darkness, it was difficult to see his eyes. But he pointed to his throat.

Pearl pulled away long enough to giggle. "Gregor doesnae speak much, if he can help it. Who have ye brought us, Citrine?"

Citrine placed one last kiss on her sister's forehead, leaving another dirty mark, then pulled away to stand beside Rory. She didn't touch him, but he was impressed by her strength, nonetheless.

"This is the Black Banner."

"The pirate?" Pearl gasped as her husband nodded to the MacLeod plaid he wore.

To his surprise, Citrine reached out and took Rory's hand. "Aye, the pirate," she said as she lifted her chin in a sign of stubbornness. "He's a good man, and I trust him."

"But William said—"

"William is dead," Rory interrupted, then pulled Citrine closer and wrapped an arm around her waist. "I killed him myself, and I would do it again."

Citrine leaned into his embrace, and he wondered how tired she was. "He was a traitor and a coward and deserved retribution."

Her sister gaped, and it was hard to tell what Gregor was thinking, but Citrine sighed. "I'll tell ye all, but might we have some food and drink?"

It was all which needed to be said; still in her nightclothes, Pearl sprang into movement, her braid swinging as she pushed her older sister into a chair at the table, commanded Gregor to fetch water, and began to slice up cold cheese and mutton.

The woman seemed to talk constantly, describing the meal they'd had the day before and how the leftovers would be just enough for them all to break their fasts—because clearly, she wasn't sleeping again this evening, and thank goodness it wasn't raining. Her silent husband lit candles, followed his wife's bidding, and watched her with a fondness that made Rory jealous.

Finally, they were all seated at the table, and Rory ate while Citrine began her tale with her voyage from Wick and the boredom she experienced…right up until pirates were sighted. She told how the pirate captain targeted her specifically, and William let him pass without challenge, which caused Pearl to gasp.

Rory interrupted with a smile. "Aye, I couldnae resist her. She fought well—better than some of my men—but was wearing a gown which hampered her." He noticed Gregor nodding proudly and assumed the man had trained with Citrine. "I eventually knocked aside her blade, tied her up, and took her and her bags with me as spoils."

"And William?" Pearl whispered.

Rory's gaze hardened. "The bastard let her go. Stood aside

and smirked as I hefted her over my shoulder like a bag of goods."

The younger woman's fingertips were on her lips, eyes wide. "Oh, Citrine. After all the two of ye shared?"

Rory thought for a moment, she was speaking of what had passed between him and his firebrand, but he only had to glance at Citrine to see that wasn't the case. Her cheeks were flushed, her gaze locked on the wee dram of whisky in her shaking hand.

Citrine and William? He suspected she was no virgin just from her enthusiastic responses to his touches, but had she and that traitor once been lovers?

Under the table, his hand clenched into a fist, and he was surprised by how jealous the realization made him.

He'd never been jealous of a partner's lovers before. But then, he'd never had a lover like Citrine before.

By St. Ninian, ye're no' quite lovers. Quit acting like she's ye're wife.

But she *was* his betrothed, wasn't she?

And when she found out who he really was, would she still want him?

It was Gregor who pushed the story forward once more. "What happened?" he rasped.

Rory startled, assuming the man never spoke, but recovered quickly. "How could I resist the allure of such a tempting prize?"

Citrine rolled her eyes. "I was terrified, aye, but Banner is an honorable man."

"Pirate," spat Gregor in that odd rasp.

Citrine shrugged. "Aye, but honorable just the same. A great leader of men, and a good man."

He felt as if he'd grown two inches. She thought that of him? It was heartening...and somehow shameful. An honorable leader of men shouldn't be a *pirate*. He should find some other way to be in command, to have control of his life.

He thought of what he'd told Citrine earlier in her chambers. About how she'd make a fine laird, given the chance, and his heart sank. He never wanted the position of laird, not with older brothers, but…he knew he would've excelled at it.

Citrine was telling the rest of their adventure: discovering Rory had the missing pearl, figuring out the meaning behind the song, and ultimately their foray into the silent keep tonight. Gregor was nodding along, but Pearl seemed to be bouncing with excitement.

As soon as Citrine ended with, "And I kenned I could come here to see ye," Pearl clapped her hands.

"Ye have the brooch? And the pearl? May I see them?"

Citrine was still carrying the box in the leather bag—that's where they'd stowed the brooch—and now she carefully opened everything. As Pearl and Gregor leaned in to examine the brooch, Rory pulled the pearl from his pouch and tumbled it across his knuckles.

He'd had it for so many years, he'd forgotten how old he'd been when he found it. A lad, certainly. The youngest in a family with too many bairns who didn't need him. He'd had it as he made his own way in the world, choosing piracy because at least it gave him the chance at control.

The smooth, white stone caught the candlelight as he rolled it across his palm, and he sighed.

He'd had it for years, but it wasn't *his*. It had never been *his*. He was only protecting it until he could get it back to its real owners.

The Sinclair Jewels.

He leaned in as well, and carefully, deliberately, placed the pearl in its spot in the brooch. Pearl sucked in a delighted breath, her silvery eyes darting to him hopefully. Rory nodded.

"'Tis yers. I'm honored to have held it for so long."

Gregor grunted—which Rory couldn't translate—but Pearl nodded reverently, eyes wide. "Ye're right," she breathed, although it was hard to tell whom she spoke to. "He *is* honorable."

Citrine sighed and scrubbed her clean hands over her sooty face, smearing the dirt more. "And now I have nae idea where to look next for the citrine. We have three of the four stones and the brooch. Mayhap I should just present them all to Da and see if he kens aught about the citrine?"

Pearl reached across the table and covered her sister's hand. "'Tis as good a plan as any. Ye can tell him of Dougal's treachery and William's accusations. Gregor will keep Da safe, I ken it, but Dougal needs to be handled."

"Aye," Citrine nodded. "Tomorrow. *Today.*" She glanced down at herself. "After I get cleaned up."

Pearl giggled and made to stand, but Gregor stopped her with a raised hand. "No' today," he rasped. "He goes to the cliffs."

From the way Citrine frowned, it was clear she wasn't the only one confused by his words. Rory turned to Pearl, in case she understood.

She nodded and sank back into her chair. "I didnae ken how frequently Da visits the cliffs near Wick, but now that I ken Gregor's schedule, I realize he goes once a month or so."

"To the cliffs?" Citrine asked with a frown.

Gregor nodded as his wife spoke for him. "He only ever takes Gregor with him but doesnae allow him to descend the path to the beach. Right, my love?" Her husband nodded stoically, and she continued. "He said 'tis a small path, and Da leaves his horse up on the cliffs and doesnae even take his sword."

Rory exchanged a glance with Citrine. "Where does he go?"

She shrugged, and Gregor matched the movement.

"He's going later today?" she asked her brother-in-law.

Gregor nodded. "Afore noon."

Citrine glanced at Rory, the question in her eyes. He nodded. "He cannae be left alone, now we ken what Dougal's capable of."

Gregor nodded, and Pearl placed her hand over his. "He willnae be."

"Aye, he willnae be alone, because I'm following him," Citrine stated firmly.

Rory's smile was grim, but he nodded as well. "And I willnae let ye go alone."

It was Pearl who broke the charged silence, jumping to her feet and clapping her hands together. "But first, ye need to get cleaned up." She whirled away from the table and hurried to a trunk in the corner of the cottage. When she straightened, she was holding a simple, blue gown, and she winked at her sister. "I dinnae have an extra set of yer trews, but I *do* have all the gowns ye didnae want to take with ye."

With a grateful laugh, Citrine rose and took the gown, along with the soap her sister offered her. "Thank ye. I've managed to go adventuring in gowns afore, and I'll do it again."

"I'll get the screen ready for some privacy while ye bathe," Pearl offered.

Gregor rasped, "Or the loch," which drew everyone's attention.

From the way Pearl blushed, the loch had special meaning to the married couple. Citrine must've realized that, too, because she chewed on her lower lip while she considered her sister and Gregor.

Rory managed not to groan aloud at the reaction to that little habit, but his cock certainly made its preference known.

Then Citrine turned golden eyes his way, and he saw his own desire reflected back. "I think the loch sounds like a fine idea," she murmured in a husky voice, and Rory knew his control was a thing of the past.

When he stood up, his kilt was clearly tented, but the sight only made her grin greedily. Gregor snorted, and Pearl giggled, but Rory didn't care about either of them. He offered his elbow, as if escorting a fine lady at court.

"The loch awaits, Lady Firebrand."

When she pressed herself against his side, he was sure sparks flew between them.

Tugging him toward the door, Citrine nodded over her shoulder to Gregor. "We'll be back here afore ye leave with Da."

The man didn't smile, but Rory thought he saw a glint of approval in his eyes. He held up a hand to pause their escape, then pulled a Sinclair plaid down from a hook on the wall. He handed it to Rory with a solemn nod, but it was his talkative wife who explained.

"On our forays to the loch, we've discovered 'tis often smart to have an extra plaid for warmth and drying."

It was Citrine who leaned around him and winked at her sister, then looked up at Rory with promise in her eyes. "Dinnae worry, Banner. I'll keep ye warm."

As the door closed on Pearl's giggles, Rory thought he might find release there in his kilt. He'd never known a woman as free and forward and certain as Citrine. She was *perfect*.

She was his betrothed, and he was lucky to be in love with her already.

But she'd called him *Banner*.

CHAPTER 13

THE EASTERN SKY was already pink, but Citrine was in no rush. She knew she had hours yet before Da would leave on his mysterious errand, and she knew just how to spend those hours. Her belly was full, she had the opportunity to bathe, and as for the man walking beside her toward the loch…?

Well, Banner was very much part of her plan to occupy herself.

She'd known him for a such a short amount of time, but there was no denying the way he made her feel. He *was* a good man, just as she'd told her sister. And the way he'd made her feel last night before William interrupted them, was like nothing she could've imagined.

Aye, she was in love with the man, which was inconvenient. He'd go back to Lewes, and she'd stay here and figure out…whatever she was supposed to do with her life.

But no reason she couldn't have a bit of fun first, aye?

When they reached the loch, Citrine pulled the gown from over her shoulder and draped it on some rocks. She'd managed to keep it clean—mostly—and didn't want it any worse from the soot which covered her clothes.

She began to unlace her tunic, but when she turned to Banner, she halted. He was just standing there, his hands in fists by his sides, *staring* at her. His eyes had a tortured look in them, and although Citrine had no idea what was causing him pain, she ached to comfort him.

"Banner?" she asked tentatively.

He swallowed, then looked away. "Go bathe, Citrine," he said hoarsely.

Her hands dropped from her laces, even though she knew her tunic and shirt were draping open alarmingly. "What is it?"

When he didn't reply, she decided it was up to her to get some answers. Boldly, she stepped toward him, halting only when they were an arm's' reach from one another. "Tell me," she commanded.

Still gazing out at the lake, Banner's reply sounded hollow. "Tell ye what?"

Lifting her hand, she placed one palm on his cheek and turned his gaze to her. "Tell me what ails ye. Please. I would help."

He closed his eyes and inhaled. "I ken what ye want, Citrine. I want it, too."

Glancing down at his tented plaid, it was very much obvious what he was referring to. She wanted to reach for that hardness, to stroke it, to guide it into her aching self…but why was he hesitating?

When she looked up at him, he was gazing into her eyes. "I've kept secrets from ye, my firebrand."

"No' the important ones. I ken who ye are."

His hand covered hers, trapping it against his cheek. "Nay. Ye dinnae. Ye've never asked my name."

His name? She scoffed. "Yer name has no bearing on yer honor or ability to lead, Banner."

He winced when she called him that. Was *that* the problem?

Fine, she'd ask him. "Would ye tell me yer real name if I asked?"

"Aye, Citrine Sinclair," he said finally. "I would. I trust ye."

He bore the name of the most notorious pirate of the Minch, and he trusted her enough with his real identity? It was humbling. "Who are ye?" she whispered.

His lovely blue eyes closed briefly, and she saw his shoulders straighten as he inhaled. When his gaze met hers once more, she saw acceptance and trust.

"I am Rory MacLeod, youngest son of the MacLeod of Lewes…and betrothed to the firebrand of the Sinclairs."

For a moment, she didn't understand.

Rory MacLeod.

She knew that name. She knew *him…*

Betrothed to the firebrand of the Sinclairs.

Rory MacLeod and Citrine Sinclair.

He was her betrothed.

She was lusting after her own betrothed.

She'd been *kidnapped* by her own betrothed.

It was such a ridiculous coincidence; she did the only thing she *could* do; she threw back her head and laughed.

And mayhap she would've gone on laughing, had his lips not crushed down on hers, his arms pulling her flush against him. The hysteria caught in her throat and turned to something else between one heartbeat and the next, then she was kissing him back with all the desperation building in her chest.

Her pelvis ground against his, her hands clawed at the skin of his back, trying to get closer, *closer*. He wound her hair around his hand, using it to take everything she was offering.

But then he tugged, pulling her back. Away from him.

They separated, gasping for air.

"Ye would laugh at me?" His tone was conversational, but there was something sincere lurking in his eyes.

Indeed, the laughter swelled once more, and she dragged one arm away from his shoulders and playfully combed through the short hair above his ears.

"Aye, I laugh, husband-to-be. From the moment I laid eyes on ye, I kenned ye were special."

"Ye were trying to kill me," he pointed out.

She shrugged, still smiling. "And I imagine the feeling will happen again sometimes."

"Ye still want to marry me?"

"I never wanted to marry ye. The youngest MacLeod son, whose name I only kenned on the betrothal contract. But then I met the Black Banner…" She dragged one fingernail through the stubble on his chin. "And I've never wanted another man the way I want him."

"Ye ken what this means, then, Citrine Sinclair?"

When he tugged on her hair, forcing her head back so she gazed up at him, desire pooled between her legs. She dared to shake her head.

He leaned even closer, his lips by her ear, and whispered, "*Ye are mine.*"

He enunciated the words with another slight tug, and Citrine felt her knees go weak.

She was a strong woman, she knew it. But this sensation of being loved by a stronger man reminded her of how she felt that first day on the pirate's birlinn. Her hands had been tied, and when he gave her a command, she'd *wanted* to obey.

"Say it," he growled.

"I am yers, Rory MacLeod."

As the words left her lips, her heart soared. It was the truth. Thanks to her father's contract, they'd be married, but thanks to a twist of fate, he held her heart.

"Always," he growled before his lips claimed hers once more.

She wanted to laugh and knew he felt the same.

She was the one who pulled away this time, gasping, "Take me, *Rory*."

His smile was satisfied, proud. "Remove yer clothes, my firebrand," he commanded.

Blessed Virgin, when he spoke to her that way, she wanted to throw herself at him, to do whatever he wanted. She made short work of tearing her tunic off, tossing it aside, and kicking off her boots. She pushed down her trews and reached for the hem of her shirt.

She only hesitated a moment before she yanked it over her head, then met his eyes with her chin raised proudly.

His gaze raked over her naked body, a look of awe and pride that made warmth pool in her belly. She pressed her thighs together, to try to capture that delicious feeling.

In two long strides, he was in front of her, his hand reaching for hers. He placed it on his belt. "Take off my kilt."

Aye!

Mayhap her hands fumbled as she worked, but soon his plaid pooled at his feet, and her hand grasped his proud, thick member. He sucked in a breath, but his gaze never left hers as his hand rose to cup her breast.

"I'm going to lay ye on the ground, Citrine. I'm going to suck on yer tits until ye scream. I'm going to put my mouth all over ye, then my cock will make ye *mine*."

She sighed at that delicious image, her head dropping back weakly. "Yers," she repeated.

His thumb brushed across her nipple. "And when I make ye mine, ye'll forget the past. Ye'll forget any other man ye once considered worthy of *this*." He cupped her other breast. "I'll plant my seed in yer womb, and we'll be joined forever."

She was halfway to ecstasy already, and he hadn't even touched her wet core. She swallowed, understanding that what he was saying was important, but her brain couldn't seem to form a coherent thought.

All she could focus on was the *promise* in his voice. "Please," she whimpered.

They fell to the plaid together, limbs tangled as they kissed and suckled and whimpered each other's names. She screamed when he fastened his lips around one nipple, and he roared her name when he finally plunged home.

Kneeling between her thighs, his powerful thrusts made her reach for his shoulders to hang on to her last shred of sanity. He was so big, so *perfect* inside her, she wanted to wrap her legs around him and keep him there forever.

And when his movements became faster, his breathing hitching, he reached between their bodies and pressed his fingers to the spot where she *needed* pressure. He'd learned that from her yesterday.

The knowledge he cared enough about her pleasure to learn from her was what sent her spiraling upward. She arched her back, forgetting to breathe as her release exploded and she uttered a wordless, choking sound.

He grabbed her hips, pulling her against him and burying his cock deep within as she felt herself pulsing around him. His own release was signaled by a flood of warmth inside her.

They held each other in silence as the sun peaked, and Citrine had to look away from the brightness.

"What?" he whispered.

"It seems right. A new day dawning."

"Aye," he chuckled, gathering her closer and pressing a kiss on her temple. "A new day."

"I ken what we shared just now, it doesnae always..." she trailed off.

When he lifted his head, she saw the question in his eyes. "What?"

"It doesnae always *have* to mean something. But I think I need to tell ye."

Now he propped himself up on his elbow. "What are ye trying to say, Citrine?"

She was making a mess of this, was she not? With a rueful shake of her head, she wrapped her arm around his middle, pulling them closer.

"I ken we're betrothed, and I ken what we just did was expected, but I think 'tis important I tell ye I *love* ye, Rory MacLeod, or the Black Banner, or whoever ye are."

She held her breath as he stared down at her, his blue eyes difficult to read. Why wasn't he responding?

Finally, he exhaled and leaned down to place a gentle kiss on her lips. "I dinnae ken how ye can love a pirate and a liar. 'Tis much easier to love a strong, intelligent, *determined* firebrand like ye."

One of her brows rose. Was he saying…?

"I love ye, Citrine, and what we just did…" He shook his head on a laugh. "What we just did most *definitely* meant something. And by the blessings of St. Ninian, it'll continue."

As if her heart wasn't swelling, wasn't soaring, at his words, Citrine faked a confused frown. "Oh, aye? Ye expect to do this again, do ye?"

He was laughing when he rolled her over and swatted at her bare bottom. "Aye, woman! After we bathe in yonder loch!"

As she pulled him to his feet, her joy slipped into her smile. "Really? Ye dinnae think ye could manage *in* the loch?"

He blinked, then a look of determination and challenge crossed his face. "Ye might wish ye hadnae said that, lass."

Laughing, she raced toward the water. "Never!"

And the man she loved followed.

CHAPTER 14

IT FELT odd to be wearing her sword belt over the blue gown Pearl had saved for her, but it was necessary. They were here to protect her father, and she couldn't do that without her weapon.

As her horse shifted, impatient, Citrine glanced over to Rory.

Rory.

He had a name now, and it was funny to think she'd once cursed that name. She'd once considered *Rory MacLeod* to be unworthy, useless as a youngest son.

Now she knew better.

Now she knew a man who chafed under his father's iron rule, who'd longed to command men of his own. He'd told her so much over the last few hours as they'd bathed in the cold loch and he'd warmed her; as they'd lain wrapped together on the Sinclair plaid Gregor had given them; as he'd helped straighten and plait her hair. He'd told her of his home and his life on Lewes, and the dreams he'd held.

Mayhap becoming a pirate hadn't been the best use of his

talents, but now that she understood the history of the Black Banner, she could understand why he had.

He'd told her about his niece and nephew, and she'd laughed to hear of Charlotte's antics. When he'd asked if the wee lass could one day travel to Sinclair lands to meet Citrine —"Ye'd be a fine role model, my firebrand," he'd said—she readily agreed, delighted at the chance to meet the little girl.

And when he'd cupped her cheeks and placed a gentle kiss on her lips, she'd nearly melted.

"I love ye," he'd whispered. "And I'll be a better man for ye. By yer side, I'll help ye save yer clan, I swear it."

And here he was. He was peering ahead, waiting for Da to start his trek down the cliffs, but when he glanced her way and saw her looking, he offered a quick grin. "No' too much longer now."

"Aye. Where do ye think he goes?"

Gregor was still atop his horse, holding the reins of Da's gelding as the older man picked his way along the path to the cliffs. The silent warrior glanced over his shoulder once, as if he knew they were watching.

Rory shrugged. "'Tis interesting Gregor doesnae ken. Ye never kenned of this journey of his?"

Citrine shook her head. "I had nae idea he was going so often. Mayhap 'tis something harmless, like a bathing pool? Or a saint's shrine?"

Grunting, Rory shook his head. "The rest of the clan would ken of it then, surely."

"Well, I guess we'll find out soon." Citrine took a deep breath. "Look, he's just disappeared down the cliffside. We'll give him another few minutes, then follow."

Nodding, Rory clucked his horse into motion beside hers. The two of them took their time approaching Gregor, but the scarred warrior turned in his saddle to nod as they neared.

Imagining her silent brother-in-law was chastising them for their tardiness, Citrine shrugged. "We didnae want to alarm him if there was nae need. I'll follow him down the trail once he's reached the bottom."

"And I'll go with ye," Rory said.

Gregor nodded, handing the reins of Da's horse to Rory. "I'll return," he rasped. "Pearl is alone."

Citrine's mind filled in the gaps of what he *didn't* say. With evidence Dougal had tried to eliminate Citrine and Pearl once, she could imagine Gregor was anxious to protect the woman he loved. She hated that he'd even had to choose between Pearl and his laird.

Wincing, she made a shooing motion. "Da is safe with us. Go make sure my niece is well."

Gregor didn't bother acknowledging her, but wheeled his horse and cantered off. Rory was watching with a wry, half-grin.

"Niece, huh?"

She shrugged. "I'm sure Gregor wants a son, but Pearl and I are hoping for a lass."

His smile grew. "Congratulations to the whole family, then. I didnae ken she was expecting."

"'Tis early yet. But Saffy is already breeding as well. Da is crowing."

His eyes dropped to her stomach, and Citrine knew what he was thinking; after what they shared over the last few hours, it was possible *she* would be breeding ere long. The thought of a bairn terrified her, especially with the future of the clan so uncertain right now. But the idea of *Rory's* bairn wasn't so horrible.

He'd be a strong wee lad with Rory's blue eyes and her honey hair, and she'd raise him to be a warrior the Sinclairs would be proud to call their own.

As soon as Dougal was dealt with.

Rory had already slid off his horse, and was tying the reins of all three animals to a post someone—Da?—had obviously installed years before. How long had he been coming here?

She followed, and soon they were peering over the edge of the cliffs. It wasn't a sheer drop, and a narrow path wound back and forth toward the beach far below. The sea was harsh today, the waves loud as they crashed against the rocks, and Citrine couldn't imagine what Da was doing down there.

"Shall we?" Rory asked playfully. At her nod, he led the way down the path.

Without having to be told, she kept an eye behind them for danger. *Dougal.*

They reached the bottom without incident, and luckily, Da's footprints were still visible in the wet sand. Rory pointed to the line of dampness on the rocks.

"We're past high tide; water's going out again. Looks like this beach would be underwater at high tide."

Following him, she nodded. "There's a stretch north of here where the fishermen put in and out. I recall my mother bringing us there a few times as bairns to swim."

"Less rocky, I assume?"

"More accessible, at least," she agreed.

Silent now, they followed Da's footprints to a gully in the sand where water drained from a crack in the cliffs toward the sea. On the other side was a beached rowboat, obviously Da's. Rory eyed the gully.

"It doesna look too deep now. A few more minutes and we might be able to wade across."

Citrine was already nodding, reaching for the ties on the shoes she'd borrowed from Pearl. She peeked up at her betrothed. "I prefer being barefoot, anyhow," she whispered.

From his smile, she could tell he agreed, and soon the two

of them were wading across the fast-flowing water. He carried their swords and belts, lifting his kilt when the water reached above their knees, and she had her hands full with her skirts. It was hard not to eye his bare backside and crack a joke, but she also didn't want to alert her father.

But once on the other side, with their weapons strapped back on, Da's footprints ended at a rock face. She frowned at Rory as the two of them examined the cliff.

He shrugged, as if to say he didn't know, but at that moment his hand pressed *into* the rock.

Jumping up beside him, she ran her hand over the bumpy surface and was surprised to discover it wasn't rock at all, but a piece of canvas cleverly painted to appear like rock. Da's footprints ended nearby, as if he'd stepped up onto one of the boulders in front of the cliff.

Why would her father be sneaking about like this?

Rory reached for the hilt of his sword, then pushed aside the canvas covering. She followed.

They stepped into a cave which stretched back some distance. The floor sloped upward, meaning most of it was dry, and voices echoed oddly up ahead. Strangest of all, though, was the fact that with the canvas replaced, it was apparent the cave was lit.

Citrine squeezed past Rory, not sure why she felt so strongly it was up to her to enter first, but he didn't prevent it. She stepped further into the cave, peeked around a jutting wall, and sucked in a breath.

The cave had been outfitted as a *home*. There were cheerful torches lighting beautiful tapestries, all done in shades of brown, white, blues, and golds. A table stood in the middle with two chairs, and comfortable cushions were strewn before a hearth. Citrine wondered where the smoke vented, and how come no one had noticed. And where did all these supplies—

food, water, and wool for the large loom which took up one wall—come from?

Her father stood in the middle of the space, speaking intently to the shrouded occupant. The person was short and wore a grey robe with an attached hood that covered whatever features Citrine might've been able to see.

"Ye *have* to let me tell them!" Duncan was saying. "Citrine is with her betrothed now, if I can trust that snake William to tell the truth of their journey. She's safe now, thank the saints, but Pearl is still here with her husband. I ken ye wanted it that way, and I can admit now ye were right. She's happy, as ye said." Her father blew out a frustrated breath and tugged at his beard. "But Dougal—"

The figure lifted a hand suddenly, cutting the laird off midsentence. Citrine nearly cursed, wanting to hear what her father would say to this hidden person. But when the shrouded head turned her way, and Da's gaze followed, Citrine decided it was time to reveal herself.

She stepped into the room, and the figure made a choking sound. Da grunted out a curse, even as he crossed the room toward her.

"What are ye doing here? Ye're supposed to be with the Black Banner."

Before she could do more than gape at him, he'd wrapped her in his arms. Then behind her, Rory cleared his throat.

"I take that to mean, Laird Sinclair, ye kenned of my identity?"

Da frowned slightly as he pulled back, his gaze going between the two of them. "No' always, but yer—I was made aware of it," he finished weakly. "What are ye doing here?"

The grey figure let out a quiet snort, which had Da scowling. "Aye, I ken," he said to the other person. "But I needed to ken she was *safe*."

"I'm safe, Da," Citrine assured him. "And my place is here, by yer side. Securing the future for the Sinclairs."

"That's what I told him."

When the figure spoke, Citrine twisted out of her father's hold to gape. It was a woman's voice. Da had been sneaking away for years…to visit a hidden woman?

"Hello, Citrine," the woman said in a low voice.

Citrine stepped toward the woman. She knew Citrine by sight? But Citrine *knew* she'd never been down here; it didn't look like many people visited the woman in this hidden grotto. So, who was she?

The woman lifted her hands to her hood, and Citrine could see her hands were wrapped in linen. It appeared as if a few fingers on each hand were missing, and when she pushed the hood back over her coif, Citrine stifled her gasp.

The woman's face had been ravaged by leprosy.

But her eyes…her eyes were familiar. They were the same bright gold as Citrine's.

A firebrand.

And Citrine *knew*. "Mother?" she whispered. Then again, "*Mother?*"

The faintest of nods from the woman told her she'd guessed correctly, and too stunned to think clearly—*Mother is alive!*—Citrine threw herself toward the woman she barely remembered.

But as soon as she moved, her mother scrambled backward, and her father shouted. "Nay!" His hand wrapped around her wrist, jerking her to a stop.

But it was Rory who hurried to her side and wrapped his arm around her shoulder, holding a shocked Citrine in place. "'Tis dangerous, Citrine," he said in a low voice. "The disease can be spread through touch."

Citrine could do little more than stare, wide-eyed, as the

woman she'd once known and loved pulled her hood back up over her coif.

Da moved to stand beside her, but didn't reach for his wife. "I'm sorry, daughter," he said in a rough voice. "I wanted to tell ye, but…"

"But I wouldnae allow him," Mother finished.

"Why?" Citrine whispered in anguish as Rory pushed her into one of the chairs at the table.

The woman—was it really Mother, after all these years?—seemed to float as she moved across the rock floor to the table and sat in the opposite chair. She didn't lift her hands again, but kept them on her lap as she stared hungrily at her daughter.

Citrine wondered what it'd be like to spend her life walled away in this place, missing her daughters and husband… She shuddered.

"I wouldnae allow Duncan to tell ye I was here," Mother began, "Because I kenned ye—of all the girls—would insist on visiting."

"Would that be so bad?" Citrine snapped, not sure if she was angry or glad Mother was sitting here speaking with her.

In response, her mother tilted her head just enough to allow the hood to fall open and reveal one hideous cheek. "Aye, my love," she whispered. "'Twould have been. Do ye think I could've refrained from holding my precious children, if ye discovered me here? Only after years without ye, have I found myself able to restrain from passing this horrible disease on."

Citrine's hands shook as she clasped them in her lap. Her mother was alive and had allowed them all to think her dead… to protect them?

"Tell me," she demanded.

Mother's chin dipped in acknowledgement as Da stepped

up behind her to mirror Rory's pose. His lips were pressed into a grim line.

The other woman took a deep breath. "Our healer discovered the disease when ye were young, and the physicians Duncan brought in confirmed it. I kenned if I wanted to protect ye all, I would have to sequester myself. If given the choice, I'd have rather gone quickly, surrounded by the ones I love, but…"

She shrugged, an awkward motion which made Citrine wonder how much was missing under the robe. "In order to save ye all—and the rest of the clan—I would have to leave. Duncan helped me build this new home, and I've been here since, with nae one but him kenning of its existence."

"And all the years, she's been here," Da growled, "She hasnae allowed a single touch."

It was obvious from the torment in his expression what he thought of that deprivation.

But Citrine understood. "Ye did it to protect us all," she whispered.

"Aye, my love." Mother nodded. "But ye have to ken that this shell of a woman ye see afore ye…I'm no' the same mother ye remember. 'Tis been too long, and I suspect I'm half-crazed as is, with yer father my only visitor."

And at high tide, the grotto would be inaccessible. A lonely existence, surely.

"What do ye…?" Citrine shook her head, unable to finish the maudlin thought.

But Mother understood. "I pray. And read." Her hood twitched slightly toward a row of shelves along the back of the cave, near the hearth. The precious books and scrolls on them would remain drier back there. "And of course, I weave."

It was then that Citrine lifted her eyes to the tapestries lining the walls. At first, she'd thought them only there to warm the room, to keep out the damp. But now she really *looked* at them.

Brown, white, blue, and gold.

There were unique designs, repeated, interlocked circles, and woven scenes. But throughout it all were those four colors.

The colors of the Sinclair jewels.

The colors of Citrine and her sisters.

A little sob caught in her throat. All these years, Mother had missed them so much, she'd surrounded herself with the memories of her children.

Rory's hands settled on her shoulders, and Citrine knew she could be strong.

Citrine met her mother's eyes—so like her own—and offered a smile through the tears. "I'm sorry, Mother. I've missed ye."

"I pray ye'll never understand how much I've missed ye, my wee firebrand," Mother whispered in a choked voice.

Da immediately reached for her shoulder, likely to offer comfort, but hesitated and pulled back at the last moment. How incredibly difficult not to be able to touch the woman he obviously still loved.

It seemed he was trying to distract himself—distract them all—when he cleared his throat. "Why are ye here, daughter?"

Citrine reached up and gripped Rory's hand and took a breath to prepare to explain. "I ken ye expected me to go to Lewes, Da, but I had nae intention of staying. Luckily— although the captain might no' see it that way—our boat was attacked by pirates, and a particularly handsome one took me prisoner."

"After ye gave him hell with yer sword, lass," Rory reminded her affectionately.

"Aye, well..." Her lips twitched. "When he heard my story, he agreed to return home with me."

Da grunted. "I ken there's more to it than that, lass. But what I meant was *why are ye here*, now? In this cave? Why did ye follow me?"

Oh. Well, time to be honest.

"Because ye're in danger, Da. We met up with William last night,"—best to leave out the details— "and he told us what I've suspected was the truth. Dougal is trying to take the laird-ship away from ye and has been trying to kill ye. He ordered William to do away with me, which is why he allowed the Black Banner to take me, and Pearl..." As she spoke, she saw her father becoming angrier and chose to get it said as fast as possible. "And the attack on Pearl was planned by William. Dougal wanted—"

"God in heaven!" Da roared, throwing up his hands and beginning to pace. "We kenned he'd try to attack me—but poison is used by weaklings! And trying to kill my daughters?" He tugged at his beard in frustration. "He'd dare to put ye in danger?"

It was Mother who spoke, her voice calm as she watched her husband's fury. "I warned ye they needed protection."

"Aye, I ken it! 'Tis why I took yer advice on all their marriage contracts!"

"Well, the ones who would *follow* their contracts, at least." There was a hint of humor in Mother's voice.

Had...had the two of them planned their daughters' marriages? Nay, it wasn't possible. But...

But Da *had* been strangely at ease with Pearl marrying one of his warriors and breaking a contract with the Sutherland. And when Saffy had disappeared for so long—to infiltrate the Sutherland holding, although Da didn't know that—he hadn't asked questions. Was it possible he'd guessed what his daughters were doing?

Or had their *mother* deduced it and told him?

Behind her, Rory cleared his throat. "'Tisnae all, Laird Sinclair. Yer daughters have assembled the jewels."

Da swung around, piercing Rory with a hard stare. But under her hood, Mother's golden eyes gleamed with excitement.

"The Sinclair jewels?" Da asked in a rough voice, his gaze dropping to Citrine. "A myth."

"Nay, Da," she assured him, reaching for her pouch. "No' a myth." Although she might not have chosen *this* moment to share the news with her father, she couldn't deny he seemed ready to act against Dougal now. Mayhap this would help.

With the others watching, she tipped the box open on the table, spilling out the tapestry, the empty brooch, and the three stones.

Mother sucked in a gasp, reaching for the pearl. Her hand hovered over the stone, two fingers and a thumb all that remained, before she exhaled and pulled her hand back.

"Are those them?" Da asked gruffly, striding around the table and reaching for the brooch. "This is the setting? Those are the missing stones?"

"Aye, Da, all but the citrine." She met his eyes. "Do ye no' see? With the jewels returned to the Sinclairs, our future is secure. We'll be strong again."

Da grunted, turning the brooch this way and that in his hand, frowning. "Tell me how this came to be," he commanded.

So, Citrine did.

With Rory's help, she recounted the events which started back with Pearl's marriage, leading through Agata's adventure with the Mackenzies, and Saffy's trip to the Sutherlands. They told her parents about Rory's finding the pearl years ago and the song which led them to the hearth in her room.

"Of *course*," Mother breathed when they finished. "The *hearthstone's view*. It makes so much sense now!"

Now? "Mother? Ye mean…"

The older woman sat in stillness for a long moment before she finally dipped her chin. "Aye, Citrine. Who do ye think gave the tapestry to Elspeth to give to ye?"

Citrine gasped, instinctively gathering the ancient tapestry closer. "Ye?"

"I've studied the stones for many, many years, and I kenned it was time for ye to gather them all."

Impossible! And yet…

Citrine's eyes strayed to the shelves of scrolls. How much of the clan's history was there? What would Saffy say about all these books to study?

Mother nodded. "I will tell ye, if ye'd like."

"Please do, Mala," Da growled. "And while ye're at it, tell me what else ye've set into motion without me kenning."

To Citrine's surprise, Mother's chuckle sounded the same as she remembered from all those years ago. "No' much, Duncan. Just events which will hopefully save our clan."

"Ye *always* say that!"

"And I've always been right, have I no'?" she challenged, lifting her chin. "When I counseled ye to allow Citrine to train with the men? Or when Pearl wanted to live among the Sinclairs, rather than far away? Ye asked for my advice then, as well as with their marriages, and we concocted a strong scheme."

Da waggled the brooch at her. "Aye, *together*. What's all this about the jewels?"

Citrine wondered if she was trying to smile behind her hood.

"I needed to give yer daughters something to do to save their clan, Duncan. Did I no'?"

With a growl, he threw up his hands. "Tell us yer story, stubborn woman!"

The older woman's chuckle stabbed at Citrine's heart, and

her hand tightened around Rory's. It was almost impossible to believe Mother was still alive, but in so many ways…she wasn't. Citrine would never be able to hug her or stroke her hair, and Mother's years of being a hermit had obviously taken a toll on her.

When she bowed her head, the hood covered everything, and with her raspy voice, it seemed believable she was merely a memory.

"Long ago, four sisters from the Campbell clan discovered their father had arranged marriage contracts for them. They were verra close, and sad to be moving so far apart."

Citrine glanced up at Rory, her heart beginning to pound faster. The four sisters Saffy had discovered! But if there were only the four, then where was the last jewel? The citrine?

"One of the sisters arrived here and married Duncan's grandda, years after his first wife had died. Yer grandfather, Citrine, was half-grown by then, and was being raised to be a fine laird. But this Campbell wife grew jealous, kenning none of the sons she bore would rise to power. So, she punished her husband's clan."

Da's knuckles tightened around the brooch. "She broke apart the Sinclair jewels."

"Aye. She broke apart the brooch and hid the jewels the only way she could imagine—sending them to her sisters."

Citrine cleared her throat. "Her sisters married into the Mackenzie, Sutherland, and MacLeod clans, did they no'?"

Mother's throaty chuckle drifted from under the hood. "I kenned ye girls would discover the truth! I'll wager it was Sapphire who studied the histories, aye? She was most like me, in that regard."

Citrine's brows rose as she glanced at her father. The Blessed Virgin knew Da was no scholar, so mayhap her scholarly twin *did* inherit that interest from their long-lost mother.

"Aye, the other Campbell sisters were spread across the

Highlands, and Lady Sinclair sent three of the jewels to them. She hid the brooch here in the keep."

Rory's weight shifted. "Was she the one who left the trail of hints? The saying, the carving, and the song? Or was that her sisters, determined not to allow the jewels to be forgotten?"

Mother's shrug showed how the disease had ravaged her body. "We may never ken. I only found two letters written from the Sutherland sister, to tell me of Lady Sinclair's jealousy and scheme. I had to infer the rest."

Da growled dangerously. "Dougal is her grandson, is he no'? The treacherous bitch believed her son should be laird, and now her grandson—"

When he bit off his words with a curse, Mother nodded. "Mayhap he inherited her goal, or mayhap he came upon it independently. But 'tis why I have warned ye all along no' to trust that man, cousin or nay."

"He's a good warrior," Da defended.

"Aye," Citrine said grimly. "And as yer cousin, he believes he has claim to the lairdship. But I'll no' let him harm ye."

Mother lifted her head once more, allowing the hood to fall back enough to pierce Citrine with those identical, golden eyes. "And after, my wee firebrand?" she rasped. "What will become of the Sinclairs?"

Somehow, Citrine knew. She *felt* her mother's blessing as it drifted over her, telling her what she wanted was right. Telling her she *could* do this.

"The Sinclairs will be strong for years to come," Citrine managed to choke out. "I *promise.*"

Da didn't understand and didn't seem to care. He slammed the brooch down on the table between them. "Brooch, agate, pearl, sapphire. Where is the citrine?"

At last, Mother moved, pushing away from the table and standing. "*Here.*"

They all seemed to hold their breath as she drifted across

the room to a large tapestry depicting four little blonde girls holding hands. When she moved it aside, Citrine saw a nook carved into the rock wall.

Her mother reached in and pulled out a large citrine. It seemed dull, until she held the stone up to the torch. Then the light hit the facets and reflected in a hundred directions, bathing the small room in golden light.

And her mother tried to smile again. "Sometimes I hold it thus and pretend it is the sun." She chuckled and shook her head, lowering the stone. "I found it here years ago. 'Twas why I remembered this cavern when I kenned it was time for me to disappear."

"Ye think the auld Lady Sinclair hid it here?" Rory asked.

"I do." Mother seemed to be having trouble breathing, and she rested her hand on the back of the chair beside the cold hearth. "I have lived here for a long time, and I have felt her malevolent presence. I believe her hatred and jealousy infected her and possibly this place. But I have fought it for many years…"

Weakly, she gestured at the tapestries as she sank into the chair, her breaths coming in gasps.

"I will no' be alive much longer, but I am glad to drag this mystery out into the open."

"Why did ye no' tell me, Mala?" Da asked in a pained voice. "I could've…"

Mother shook her head. "This was for yer daughters, Duncan Sinclair. They are the clan's future, and they needed to ken that."

Suddenly, Citrine understood what her mother was hinting. She stood, pushing the chair back but keeping her hold on her betrothed's hand.

"Dougal will pay for his sins."

Da shook his head as if putting aside the mystery of the jewels, not realizing how closely they were tied to the clan's future. "Ye're right, lass," he growled. "He had the audacity to threaten my life, but to discover he's been threatening my bairns? He'll die for that crime."

Rory stepped up beside her. "We dinnae ken who is loyal to him, who has higher aspirations."

"It doesnae matter!" Da slammed his fist into his palm. "We'll root them all out, then worry about the future!"

"Take the jewels, Citrine," Mother said in a weak voice, holding out the last stone. "They are the proof ye need of yer worthiness. Only the cleverest and bravest of the Sinclair warriors could've retrieved them."

It felt as if she were in a trance. Citrine's bare feet padded softly across the cold stone of the chamber, until she stopped before her mother. She crouched down and held out her hand.

Mother leaned forward as if to touch her, but sucked in a breath and halted. Slowly, carefully, she dropped the last of the Sinclair jewels into Citrine's palm.

"I love ye, my daughter."

"I love ye, too, Mother."

Her mother sat back with a sigh. "Go now," she commanded. "Make Dougal pay. Win yer future. I'll be here when ye're done, I swear it."

Full of grim determination, Citrine stood and whirled, her sword slapping against her thigh, filling her with confidence.

"Da?"

Her father grunted, his own hand falling to his sword's hilt.

Rory finished setting all the jewels into the brooch, bending the prongs to hold them. When she tossed the citrine to him, he added that one as well, then slid the completed brooch into the pouch. He tied it closed, then handed it to her, leaving the box and tapestry on her mother's table.

"Ye carry these, Citrine," he said in a low voice.

She nodded, a sense of surety filling her. This was *right*. "Ye stand behind me on this, husband-to-be?"

His lips twitched upward. "Nay, my love. I stand *beside* ye. Where I belong."

Nay, it wasn't just *right*…it was *perfect*.

"Well?" Da growled from the canvas-covered door. "Let us go kill a traitor!"

Citrine glanced once at the shrunken figure in the chair. Her mother—or the person who'd once been her mother, at least—nodded her blessing, and Rory's hand slid into Citrine's.

"Aye," Citrine said as she lifted her chin. "Let us secure the future of Clan Sinclair!"

CHAPTER 15

Duncan Sinclair's voice rang through the training yard, halting fights and causing his men to turn his direction. Rory knew Citrine had spoken of her father's illness, but it didn't seem to affect him now. In fact, he looked strong as an ox, striding toward his commander.

Citrine exchanged glances with Rory, and the two of them followed. He couldn't help but notice her hand was on her sword's hilt, same as his.

They were ready for anything.

Although he probably had no right to feel this way, he was inordinately proud of her. Only hours ago, she'd discovered her mother—the woman she'd mourned—was still alive. Granted, living in that hidden grotto as a hermit hardly counted as "alive", but it was remarkable, nonetheless. And to discover not only was Mala Sinclair still alive, but she'd been subtly influencing her daughters' futures through her meetings with the laird…it was hard to take in.

Rory was reeling, so he could only imagine what Citrine was feeling right now.

But her expression didn't show any of it. She kept her chin high in that stubborn way of hers, and her golden eyes flashed with fire in the noon sun as she glared toward her father's cousin, who slowly straightened from where he'd been showing a block to a younger man.

As Rory strode beside his betrothed, he eyed the men surrounding them. Duncan was leading them into the center of a mass of Sinclair warriors. Warriors who should be loyal to their laird, but who'd spent years training with Dougal.

Whose side would they choose, when Duncan challenged his commander?

The Sinclair laird halted in the middle of the yard, and Citrine moved to stand beside him. Rory stepped up to his other side, but angled his body to keep as many of the other men in his sight as possible.

"Dougal Sinclair!" the laird bellowed. "I kenned ye were up to nae good. I *kenned* ye wanted my position when I was gone!"

Frowning, Dougal pointed the tip of his sword at the ground, the sun reflecting off the sweat on his shoulders, reminding Rory he'd be tired…but ready to fight.

"Aye, and what of it, *cousin*? I am yer closest male relative."

"But no' my *son.*"

Dougal shrugged. "Ye have nae sons, auld man. And yer daughters cannae be laird after ye."

Before Duncan could speak, Rory did. "Why no'?" When all eyes turned his way, likely wondering who he was, he shrugged innocently. "Why can one of the Sinclair Jewels no' be laird? If she were strong and capable?"

Dougal scowled, nodding to Citrine. "I suppose ye speak of this unnatural bitch—"

Duncan took control of the conversation once more, stepping forward to interrupt. "Ye were no' content to wait though, were ye? Ye thought to help me along. *Murder*," the older man spat. "Murder is never the honorable way."

Around them, mutterings began, and Rory found himself praying that was a good sign. If the Sinclair warriors weren't aware of Dougal's attempts, then that meant they didn't support his bid for the lairdship. Right?

For his part, Dougal said nothing. But his frown grew as he glared at Duncan, whose face was turning red from anger. The older man's hand didn't leave the hilt of his sword, but he jabbed a finger from the other hand toward his cousin, rage in his eyes.

"And if *poisoning* me wasnae enough, ye try to murder my *daughters*? Ye thought to marry one, and if that didn't work, to eliminate them?" He scoffed. "So, ye *are* afraid a woman could hold this position? Ye thought to remove them from yer path?"

"What's this, then?" someone called from the crowd.

"Murder? Dougal?" another shouted. "Our wee lasses?"

Rory could see Duncan was too angry to think clearly. He could confront Dougal, but without the support of his warriors, he'd eventually lose. Holding up his hands, Rory lifted his voice to be heard by the gathered crowed.

"'Tis true! Dougal was behind the attack on Pearl when she traveled south. Ye remember the bandits who ambushed them, and the Hound rescued her?" He waited until he heard the grunts of agreement from the men around him, then pointed to their commander. "*Dougal* gave the orders to arrange it, to contact the lawless bandits. He kenned how much good Pearl did for the clan—did for ye, and yer wives and bairns and families—and kenned she needed to be removed far from home. Living here, she'd always be a danger to him, by dint of her bloodline."

When he mentioned the good sweet Pearl did for the clan, the men's nods turned to anger, and by boldly stating Dougal's sins, Rory was hoping to turn them to outright rage against their commander. Judging from the way they scowled at Dougal, it was working.

"Lies!" the commander bellowed, his other hand wrapping around his sword's hilt. "This is all lies!"

"Nay!" Rory called before Duncan could. He *knew* he could control this crowd, these men. It was what he'd been born to do, the reason he'd found fulfillment at sea. "Nay, and we have a confession! William, one of ye!" His gaze swept the gathered men, watching as they began searching for the young man. "William, who'd once fancied himself a match for one of the Sinclair Jewels, aye? But was naught but a weak coward. Ye ken him!"

"Where is he?" someone called.

"Always kenned he was bitter about no' being good enough!" came another voice, and others nodded or called out their agreements.

"Aye!" Rory turned so he could address all the men at once. "*William*, who was assigned to the guards who went south with Pearl. Two good men—yer friends, men ye've fought beside—died in that attack!" Rory couldn't recall their names, but he wouldn't admit that right now. "But wee William conveniently survived, returning home a hero, aye?" He didn't wait for their agreements, before continuing, "'Twas *he* who told of the attack and of Pearl's adventure...but *he* who arranged it all, on Dougal's orders!"

"Lies!" Dougal said again, but with less conviction. He was eying the men around them, as if judging how much they believed. "I've never confessed to this!"

"Ye didnae have to!" Rory bellowed, gaining the men's attention. He saw Citrine glance at him, an approving glint in her eyes, before she went back to studying the crowd. Interestingly, Duncan looked content to have Rory hold the crowd's attention.

"Ye didnae have to," Rory repeated, not even looking at

Dougal, "because William confessed it all. He told how Dougal promised him the position of commander when Dougal was laird…when he became laird by dishonorably *murdering* Duncan!"

He waited for the jeers to begin, and as soon as Dougal opened his mouth to deny it, Rory hurried to interrupt him.

"And 'tisnae all! William—that same, sniveling cowardly traitor—was in charge of Citrine's safety, aye? Yet he returned here just days ago, telling of her capture by pirates? What he likely didnae mention was he stood by and let their captain *kidnap* her! Didnae even lift his sword to protect her!"

Outraged mutters began again, and Citrine stepped forward. "'Tis true," she called loudly, capturing everyone's attention. "He allowed the notorious Black Banner to take me off that ship, and I might've been going to my death. But 'twas his *plan*! He confessed all, aye, and told us if the pirates hadnae stolen me, Dougal had ordered him to kill me on the way to Lewes."

"Nay!" and "That bastard!" rang out among the gathered men. "Ye fought bravely, lass!" someone called.

"Aye," she agreed, not at all arrogantly, "And I would've fought *him*, had I kenned. But this man, my betrothed"—she pointed proudly at Rory—"by my father's own hand, saved me. Rory MacLeod of Lewes, also a sailor, *saved me*, while William was willing to let me die, by Dougal's orders. And for what?"

When she spat on the ground, more than a few of her father's warriors did the same, and Rory knew they were loyal to Duncan and his family. All the sneaking around for the last day had been unnecessary, had they known whom the Sinclair warriors would follow.

"The lad was promised a position of power," Rory growled. "But the real traitor stands afore ye!"

Dougal had actually backed up a step, a conflicted expression on his face. He was glancing to both sides, but it was impossible to tell if he was looking for a way out or hoping for more support.

And he still hadn't confessed.

"Where is William?" someone called from the back of the crowd, and others took up the question.

Rory lifted his hand once more. "Ye'll find him north of here, at the edge of the patrols' range. He was alone when we found him, and he tried to finish what he'd failed to do…kill Citrine." With his other hand, he patted his sword. "I didnae allow it."

It wasn't said smugly, but there were more than a few approving grunts from the warriors.

Citrine called out, "If anyone besides the carrion birds want to ken where his body lies, I'll show them after this is over." She faced Dougal squarely, challenge in her eyes. "I spat on his body, and I'll do the same for yers when ye lie dead at my feet for what ye've done, *cousin*."

The reactions of the gathered men ranged from approval to concern. One older man crossed his arms over his chest and scowled, while two others called out encouragement.

Rory, however, felt as if he'd been kicked in the chest. God's blood, what was she doing?

"In light of yer crimes against my family, I challenge ye, Dougal Sinclair, for the position of laird's heir!"

Well, shite.

Frantic, Rory exchanged glances with Duncan. Her father didn't look alarmed; if anything, he seemed at ease with the idea of his daughter challenging an older, more experienced warrior. Was he smiling? Nay, surely it was just a show of confidence?

By His wounds, the men were actually backing up, giving the combatants space? Rory turned in a circle, trying not to let his concern show, as it became obvious—despite their grumbles or support, the Sinclair warriors were *going to let Citrine fight the bastard*!

Desperate now, Rory managed to catch Citrine's attention. He couldn't forbid this fight, nay, but surely…surely *something* could be done? Could he fight in her place? He did his best to show her—to *beg* her—and she understood. She *must've* understood, but she gave a little shake of her head to let him know she wasn't going to back down.

Damnation.

Taking a deep breath, Rory knew there was nothing he could do. By speaking against this match, he'd be denying her his support.

He squeezed his eyes shut momentarily, then took a deep breath and met her fiery gaze once more. *"I love ye,"* he whispered, knowing she wouldn't be able to hear him.

Mayhap she read his lips, or mayhap she was thinking the same thing, because she nodded…and smiled.

God help him, but he was going to have to stand by and watch the woman he loved battle a warrior.

To no one's surprise, Dougal was grinning evilly as he made a show of limbering up his muscles and stretching his shoulders. When Citrine finally looked his way, he gestured imperiously. "I'll gladly prove my worthiness as the next Sinclair, but killing a wee *lass* will no' do it."

To her credit, Citrine didn't blanche or even look nervous at his casual words. Instead, she scoffed. "So, ye're backing out of the challenge? Can I be the first to call ye coward?"

"Nay," Dougal growled, lifting his sword. "Ye've called me murderer and traitor today, but ye'll no' call me coward. I'll kill ye for that, *bitch.*"

Instead of reacting to his taunt, Citrine shrugged as she reached between her legs and pulled up her skirts to tuck them into her sword belt, making an awkward pair of trews. "I still call ye traitor, but without yer confession, I'll make do with calling ye a *failed claimant* to my father's position." She pulled out her sword and settled into the ready position.

Dougal spat on the ground, showing her what he thought of her claims, and the men around him murmured disapproval. Then Rory stopped caring what the crowd was doing, because Dougal attacked.

He gave no indication, just flashed into action. Citrine got her sword up in time to block, but it was clear he didn't intend to go easy on her. By Dougal's third blow, it became apparent that he was by far the stronger of the two opponents, and Citrine was struggling to block each strike.

It took everything in Rory not to step forward, to draw his own sword, and save her. His knuckles were white, he was gripping his hilt so tightly, and he held his breath as he followed the battle before him.

Luckily, Citrine had trained with larger men. He remembered his fight with her on the deck on the birlinn, and then later their sparring session; she was not only a willing and capable student, but she'd learned plenty of moves to account for her smaller stature.

Still, that knowledge—even watching her—didn't make Rory feel any better about what he was seeing.

Citrine leaped and twisted around her larger opponent, ducking his blows and coming in from unexpected angles. She didn't so much throw off his strikes as move away from them; so, their blades would engage, but then suddenly she just *wasn't there* anymore.

There was a moment when she'd fallen back, that Dougal didn't attack again. Instead, he shook his head, not even breathing heavy. "Ye think to use my own moves against me, bitch? I *taught* ye everything ye ken!"

Citrine *was* breathing heavy, but she shrugged. "No' *everything.*"

And then *she* attacked.

God's blood!

She was a vision, an angel—a *jewel*—striking against Dougal. Her hair glowed gold in the sunlight, and her gown matched the color of the clear sky.

I taught her that move!

She was a firebrand, and Rory would be damned if he'd let Dougal harm her.

He was already stepping toward the battle when he glanced at her father. The laird was frowning now, as he should be, his eyes flicking between his daughter and his cousin. Rory paused, waiting for the old man to stop this battle, but Duncan kept his lips pressed closed.

Rory might not understand the man's actions, but he understood his own feelings. He'd protect the woman he loved.

And he'd have the chance.

Before he'd gone more than two steps, Citrine's luck ran out.

She was twisting, ducking under one of Dougal's strikes with far more power than she could hope to block…and her gown loosened. When she stepped sideways, her foot caught in her skirts and, unbalanced, she began to fall.

The world seemed to slow as Rory watched her throw out her hand to counter-balance herself. Dougal's lips curled into a savage grin as he saw his opponent's opening and lifted his blade for a finishing blow. And Rory wouldn't get there in time.

But he'd try.

In one move, he leapt toward the pair and drew his sword, bellowing his war cry to distract Dougal.

"Beware the Black!"

It worked.

Dougal jerked at the sound, halting his strike long enough to assess the new danger, just as Citrine hit the ground. That pause likely saved his life, because Rory was prepared to stab the man in the back to protect her. But Dougal managed to raise his blade enough to catch Rory's, stumbling back in the process.

Dimly, Rory registered the calls and jeers from the men around him, but he had no time to listen. Instead, he focused on Dougal, and wished like hell for Bull's strength or Bartholomew's wit.

Nay.

He was alone here, without his loyal men.

Ye have Citrine.

And that was enough. He had her, and he would *keep* her. With a growl, he threw off Dougal's block and began to harass the other man. He didn't have the commander's experience, aye, but he was younger and stronger.

And he was the Black Banner, by God.

He *would* protect Citrine.

Dougal's blocks were becoming slower, and Rory used his age against him, forcing the older man to move constantly to protect his sides as well as his front. Years spent battling onboard a ship had honed Rory's balance, and he used it all— plus his strength—to his advantage.

As outmatched as Citrine had been against Dougal, it was soon clear Rory would win this bout.

But *should* he?

This was Citrine's fight.

He halted in his attack for a moment, giving up an advantage to risk a glance at where she'd fallen.

She wasn't there.

But Rory didn't have the time to look for her, because Dougal took advantage of his distraction to launch his own attack, bellowing wordlessly as he threw himself toward the younger man.

Lifting his blade in time, Rory caught the other man's

sword against his weapon and, knowing he had the stronger position, threw it off. But before he could lunge forward, Dougal's sword swept toward his knees.

Cursing his own distraction, Rory leapt back, managing to keep his balance *and* his sword up. Which was good, because Dougal used his momentum to bring another crushing blow toward Rory's neck.

Rory's blade caught the other man's, but it was to be a contest of strength.

Then, from the corner of his eye, he saw a flash of gold and blue.

Before he had a chance to call a warning, Citrine was there, ducking under their raised arms, and shoving the blade of her shorter sword deep in Dougal's chest.

The man's eyes widened as his mouth opened. No sound emerged, but when he coughed weakly, blood leaked down his chin.

Then, slowly, he stumbled backward, his hands still gripping his sword. As his knees gave out, he fell to his side on the ground, coughed again, then was still.

Panting, Citrine straightened and met Rory's eye. "I'll no' apologize."

He remembered how to breathe. "What?"

"I'll no' apologize for killing him. I *will* thank ye for saving my arse when the stupid gown tripped me, but it was my challenge."

Rory's blood was still pounding in his ears, his vision still tinged red at the edges. He forced himself to breathe deeply, to try to push aside the terror he'd felt when she'd tripped.

It didn't work.

With a snarl, he reached out with his free hand and grabbed the back of her neck. Before she could object, he'd pulled her closer, slamming his lips down on hers.

She welcomed him, opening her mouth with an erotic little moan of surrender, and wrapping her arms around his neck.

St. Ninian alone knew how long they stood there in one another's arms, breathing each other's air and reveling in the knowledge *they were alive*. For Rory, a million heartbeats—a million *lifetimes*—could've passed, or a blink of an eye. All he knew was this was right, this was *perfect*, and he would never, ever let her go.

Eventually, the sound of cheering broke through the perfect cocoon he'd wrapped around himself, and he felt her smile against his lips. He pulled away just far enough to rest his forehead against hers, his sword still dangling from his other hand. When she tightened her hold on his neck and smiled, he slowly exhaled.

"I love ye," she whispered.

"And I love ye," he replied. "But do no' *ever* ask me to stand by and watch ye battle for yer life again, no' without helping ye."

"Ye did help me," she pointed out with a smirk.

"Aye, but I did my best to allow ye yer challenge first." He shook his head slightly, then pressed himself against her once more. "Christ Almighty, Citrine, do ye ken what that did to me, to watch ye fight him? To watch ye *fall*?"

Around them, the sounds of stomping, metal banging against metal, and cheering seemed to form a wall around them, but Citrine's fiery eyes burned up at him.

"I'll no' ask ye again, my love. But only if ye swear to stand beside me on everything."

"I swear it," he said fervently. "I'd even stand in front of ye, if ye'd allow it."

She chuckled. "And I'd stand in front of ye for the same reason. I would protect ye if I could."

"I'm a pirate, love. I need nae protection."

"Nay." Her lips brushed against his. "Ye're a laird's husband."

He'd just begun to chuckle when something slammed into his back.

As he spun, he tucked Citrine against his hip and lifted his sword, prepared to shove her aside if necessary. A thought flickered through his mind that she wouldn't appreciate him protecting her this way, but he could buy her time to retrieve her sword from Dougal's chest and—

Thank Christ Rory had years of experience on a pitching deck, because he managed to halt his movements in time, *and* keep from falling over when a beaming Duncan slapped him on his back a second time.

"Whoa, lad, I see yer blood is still boiling, aye?" The older man laughed. "After a fight like that—a *kiss* like that!—I can imagine!"

"Da," Citrine groaned, dropping her forehead to Rory's shoulder, "go away."

"No' a chance, daughter!" Duncan was still chuckling when he turned to his men and raised his hand for silence. It took a bit, but eventually the gathered warriors elbowed one another to attention. "Ye all understood what happened here, aye? A challenge was issued and met."

Citrine straightened as the men nodded in agreement, some more enthusiastically than others. "Aye! I ken ye never thought to have a woman as a laird, but I am my father's most logical choice of his offspring, and by losing, Dougal forfeited no' just his life, but his right to the position."

A voice from the crowd rang out, "But ye didnae beat him."

Citrine glared as if trying to figure out who had spoken. "I didnae beat him *alone*. But 'twas my sword that took his life."

Before the man could taunt her into an argument, Rory lifted his chin. "I helped her, aye. When my betrothed—the woman I love—was in danger, I stepped up to help. Who among ye would do differently?"

When the men began to mutter and nod, he shot Citrine a glance to ask her to let him handle this. She'd called him a leader of men; let him use that skill.

"Aye, I helped her. I engaged Dougal in combat, while she recovered. But 'twas *her* blade which ended his life. 'Twas *her* blade which removed a coward and a traitor from the Sinclair ranks." He nudged Dougal's body with his foot, then spat on it. "And 'tis her blade that remains in his wicked heart."

The rumblings turned to outright jeers and calls of agreement, as Rory sheathed his sword. He held up one hand for silence and reached for Citrine with his other. "I am no' a Sinclair warrior, but I hope ye'll accept me as one of yer own. I left Lewes to captain a ship, and I'll confess I was angered to learn my father had bartered me away on a marriage contract I didnae want." He smirked down at Citrine, who rolled her eyes at him, to the men's laughter. "But then I *met* my firebrand here, I decided mayhap my father and Laird Sinclair kenned what they were doing."

Over the laughter, Rory lifted his voice. "Citrine is a strong warrior and an intelligent leader, but she could no' defeat Dougal alone. Nay, ye saw that. I have nae claim to Sinclair lands, but I *do* claim a Sinclair's heart. As long as she—and Clan Sinclair—will have me, I'll stand beside her and protect her and these lands with my blade, my life, and my heart."

That declaration earned a roar of approval from the gathered men, and Citrine tugged his lips down to hers. She brushed a kiss across them, then murmured, *"Thank ye."*

"Together we are stronger, my love," he whispered in response and knew she'd understood when her lips tugged into a smile.

It was the laird himself who stopped the celebration, waving his hands over his head to gain everyone's attention.

"Shut yer mouths, ye lot! Ye havenae heard the best part! Shut up!"

As the men quieted once more, Duncan hooked his thumbs into his sword belt and rocked back on his heels, a smile on his face. He took a deep breath and launched into a booming tale.

"Generations ago, we Sinclairs had a brooch, the symbol of our power, aye?" He didn't wait, but hurried on with the story. "But a witch of a woman—Dougal's grandmother, actually—married my grandda and grew jealous of the Sinclair power. Thinking to weaken the clan so her own sons could claim it, she stole the brooch and divided up the jewels, sending them to her kin across the Highlands."

The men's reactions ranged from anger to laughter, clearly disbelieving the story. But Duncan continued.

"These sisters she sent the jewels to, they werenae as cold-hearted as Dougal's grandmother. They didnae let the story die, but passed the legend down to their children through clues and hints. But it would've ended there, had nae one thought to search for these clues."

"And now, Chief?" someone called. "Ye've found the jewels again?"

"No' I," boomed Duncan, his smile resting on Citrine. "The legend said only the most skilled and bravest Sinclair warrior would be able to return the jewels to the Sinclairs. *That* warrior is fit to lead the clan with a strong man by her side."

The mutterings increased as the men realized who Duncan was talking about. Rory squeezed her shoulders and grinned down at Citrine.

"Ye'd better show them, love."

She shrugged out of his hold and scrambled for her leather satchel, pulling out the pouch he'd wrapped the brooch in. He watched her take a deep breath, then shove her hand into the air, turning to allow all the gathered men the chance to see the jewels.

The sun caught the facets of the sapphire and citrine, throwing blue and gold light across the crowd, while the agate and pearl shone beautifully. As one, the gathered men sucked in reverent breaths.

And as Citrine slowly turned, showing the face of the Sinclair jewels to all those gathered, a warrior sunk to one knee. Another followed, then another, until all the gathered men—the might of the Sinclairs—knelt before her. Rory wasn't sure if they were saluting the return of the brooch, or her right to lead the clan, but the respect they showed was humbling.

Stepping up beside Duncan, Rory knew he couldn't leave this unsaid. "Ye pledged yer loyalty to yer clan and yer history. Ye fought bravely for Duncan, even kenning the Sinclair jewels were missing. Now that they've returned?" He didn't wait for their confusion to clear, but pushed on. "Will ye acknowledge Citrine Sinclair, the warrior brave and cunning enough to no' only collect and return the jewels to their rightful home, but weed out the traitor in our midst, as yer leader?"

The men's "Ayes!" were deafening.

Rory turned to Duncan, and when he saw the twinkling in the man's eyes, offered his hand. The laird clasped his forearm.

"I'll be pleased to call ye son-in-law. Seems yer father and I kenned what we were doing, eh?"

Rory smiled in return. "Aye, and I swear I'll make Citrine happy."

"I trust her enough to ken how to deal with ye if ye didnae, lad!" He snorted and shook his head, still smiling. "But what ye said was the truth. Ye're what Citrine needs, no' only as a husband but a partner. I dinnae intend to die for many a year, but when I do, I'll be happy kenning I'm leaving the Sinclairs in both yer hands."

Feeling his throat close up with emotion, Rory could manage little more than a nod and a choked, "Thank ye, Laird Sinclair."

And then Citrine was between them, her arms around his neck, and Duncan was moving away to laughter and slaps on his back.

Rory grinned down at his betrothed. "Ye did it," he murmured. "Ye returned the jewels and saved yer father. Ye brought a future to the Sinclairs."

Her eyes seemed to sparkle even more than usual, and that's when he realized they were bright with unshed tears. Still, her smile was perfect.

"I couldnae have done it alone, Rory. No' only did ye help me defeat Dougal, but ye gave us the pearl. I'd only have three of the stones, even if I'd followed Da to discover my mother. Ye're the reason we have all four."

With his hands on her hips, he pulled her up against him. "A fortnight ago I was watching my niece Charlotte playing and bemoaning the fact my wife would never match her spirit. Who would've thought, when I saw that merchant ship, I'd meet no' only my betrothed, but the woman I'd love?"

With a mischievous glint in her eyes, she shifted her hips against his, and when his cock invariably gave an eager jump, smirked up at him.

"Aye, and a fortnight ago *I* was complaining to my sister that I'd no' marry the youngest son of some far-off laird who lived on a smelly island." She grinned. "I told her I dinnae even like fish, which is the truth!"

Chuckling, he shook his head. "Lent must be miserable around here."

She tugged lightly on the hair at the back of his neck. "What I meant was that I'd nae intention of living on Lewes. I was going just long enough to find the stone hidden there and return. Ye cannae imagine my surprise when I saw ye pull the pearl out as if it were naught more than a bauble."

"I think I can," he murmured, remembering the expression on her face. "And ye were so *angry*."

"I was ready to give myself to ye that day."

When she flushed slightly after her admission, Rory realized what she'd meant, and his cock jumped again.

"Ye mean in exchange for yer jewels? All I wanted was a kiss."

"Aye, I ken that now, but ye were a *pirate*. I expected the worst."

Pressing his hips forward, making sure she knew *exactly* how much he wanted her, he brushed a kiss against her lips. "I am honorable," he murmured. "But only so far. Ye can tempt a pirate *or* a priest."

Grinning, she wriggled again. "Ye're a pirate nae longer, husband-to-be. The Black Banner will have to retire, if ye hope to rule by my side."

"I ken it." When she ground against him again, he stifled a groan and dropped his forehead to hers. "'Twill nae be a hardship, lass, but my men will have to decide if they want to serve the next Black Banner or return home."

"They're welcome to come to Sinclair lands."

"Aye," he gasped, "I'll tell them so."

Around them, the celebration continued as Duncan promised his men ale and the full tale that evening at supper. But Rory's world had shrunk to the fiery eyes before him and the perfect woman in his arms who grinned so mischievously.

"Then I think we've settled all but one important matter," she said in a teasing tone.

God's blood, but it was hard to think when he was this aroused. "Aye?"

"Aye." Her tone turned serious. "I think we need to go back to my chambers and lock the door so we cannae be disturbed."

He knew what he *wanted* her to say, but teased her right back. "So we can keep looking for more hints about the jewels?"

"Nay." She winked and pulled his head down toward hers. "So ye can investigate how easy it is to make love to me in a gown for a change."

He burst out laughing just as her lips claimed his, and he knew in his heart he was where he belonged.

EPILOGUE

A YEAR LATER...

"I CANNAE BELIEVE we're all together again!"

Citrine reached for Agata's hand, squeezing it just to reassure herself she was really there. Their oldest sister had the longest journey home, which is why this was her first visit since marrying the Mackenzie regent last summer. She'd arrived two days ago, and Citrine had so enjoyed catching up with her.

Agata squeezed her hand in return. "I never doubted it would happen, but I'm thrilled the weather cooperated, and we have so much to celebrate!"

The two of them smiled across the room, to where Pearl was chatting animatedly with a slender young woman—Merrick's natural daughter, Mary, and her husband. Pearl was patting the bottom of her infant daughter, one of the reasons they had all gathered.

"Do ye think she'll bring her over here?" Agata's husband

Jaimie was watching the bairn with a hint of wistfulness on his scarred face. "She's such a sweet little angel."

Agata released Citrine's hand and wrapped her arm around her stepson Callan's shoulders as she smiled indulgently at her husband. "Ye didnae get enough of holding her yesterday?"

Shrugging, Jaimie looked a little sheepish. "I'm as surprised as ye are to discover I'm quite enamored of wee bairns."

For as long as Citrine could recall, Agata had dreamed of a husband and children to care for. This oldest Sinclair Jewel was the heart of them all; the one who'd held them together and cared the most. She, more than anyone, deserved a houseful of bairns to care for, and it seemed as if mayhap her husband felt the same way.

Citrine wanted to ask but wasn't sure if the topic was appropriate for eight-year-old Callan. "Have ye played with yer cousins yet?" she asked him, nodding across the room to where Merrick Sutherland's brood were cavorting, their nurse frazzled and overworked as she tried to keep up with them all.

Merrick and Saffy had hired extra help to control all his children, but they were still rambunctious as ever. Interestingly, since their marriage, no new Sutherland bastards had shown up at their doors, although Saffy seemed strangely at ease with the knowledge it might happen again. Citrine knew there was more to the story than she understood but didn't need to learn Merrick's secrets.

Callan snorted politely. "I have, thank ye. 'Tis a bit overwhelming."

Bursting into laughter, Citrine had to agree. "Very diplomatic, Laird Mackenzie," she admitted with a slight bow, which made the boy smile. "I imagine 'tis a surprise to go from being an only child to having a dozen cousins."

The lad shrugged. "I dinnae mind all of them. Adelaide seems quite nice and studious, but she's so *old*. Maggie and Becks and Nolan and the others are too rambunctious. The younger ones are aright, I suppose." He shrugged, then looked up at his uncle. "Aunt Pearl let me hold wee Mala yesterday for a while, and I liked her verra much. She doesnae speak, ye ken."

Jaimie nodded solemnly at his nephew. "A verra important character trait when choosing friends."

"Aye." The lad puffed out his chest. "Besides, I have to learn how to care for a bairn. Agata taught me how to keep my hand under her head." He lowered his voice conspiratorially. "I have to ken these things, ye understand, for when *my* bairn arrives."

Thinking the lad was already considering his adult years, Citrine began to chuckle. But when she noticed her sister's blush, she caught her breath.

"Agata! Does he mean what I think he means?"

With a small smile, Agata reached for her husband's hand. Jaimie was beaming proudly.

"Aye," he rumbled. "We werenae sure 'twould ever happen, but our prayers have been answered."

"Praise God," Citrine whispered, tears coming to her eyes.

"For what?" Rory startled her when he slipped his arms around her from behind. "Why are we all looking so shocked over here?"

Callan lifted his chin. "I'm going to be a big brother, Uncle Rory. Aunt Citrine is a bit overwhelmed, so be polite, please."

The wee lad's serious tone made Citrine smile through her tears, and as she reached for her sister to hug her, Rory offered Jaimie his hand. "Congratulations!" The other man wrapped his ruined hand around Rory's forearm, both of them beaming.

"And how about ye?" Agata whispered, holding Citrine close. "I ken ye have duties, but when will ye be having a wee one to follow?"

Citrine exchanged a glance with Rory. They'd spent the last year ensuring they *wouldn't* have a child, just because of their new responsibilities. They'd traveled so often in the last twelve months, she couldn't imagine having a bairn as well.

Taking a deep breath, she tried to explain it to her older sister. "I ken it needs to happen. The clan will be settled much better if I have a few sons to follow after us when we're in charge. But we're just no' ready yet."

Nodding, Agata leaned back. "I understand. But ye should consider it before Da is gone. No' only does he adore bairns, but 'twill be much easier to raise them before the two of ye have to take over yer full duties as laird."

Citrine reached for Rory's hand, and he slipped into her embrace easily. "Aye, we've considered that. Sometime in the next year or so, mayhap, because Da is healthier than ever."

"I'm glad to hear it." Agata smiled. "I couldnae believe it, when I read yer letter explaining everything which had happened."

"'Tis true," Jaimie offered. "We had to re-read it many times."

"I helped with the hard words," Callan offered.

At that, Rory began to chuckle. "I ken ye must be inundated with cousins, but I have two I want ye to meet. My niece Charlotte and nephew Tavish were here for Hogmany. They're a bit younger than ye, but I'll see if I can talk their father into sending them for another visit when ye're here one day."

Jaimie grinned. "Or ye can all return to Mackenzie lands for another visit with us." Citrine and Rory had traveled there last autumn. "Because Lewes is much closer to our home than yours!"

Nodding, Rory hummed thoughtfully. "'Tis a good idea. I *did* promise a visit home this summer, but we were planning to go by birlinn…"

He glanced across the hall to where his friend Bartholomew was playing with Merrick's brood, and Citrine knew her husband was remembering his time at sea.

A year ago, he'd promised to give up pirating, and he had. More than a few stories had risen in the Western Isles about the Black Banner's disappearance, each more fantastic than the last. She suspected Rory had something to do with that, spreading rumors and fantastical tales whenever possible.

But she knew her husband missed sailing. They were lucky enough not to have to fully accept leadership yet, although Rory often helped train the men with Gregor, who'd been made commander after Dougal's death. The two men worked well together; Gregor had the experience, and Rory had the leadership skills necessary to win the warriors to his way of thinking.

It was those same skills which had made him such a successful captain. Whenever they could, Rory and Citrine would sneak away to the coast, to sail in one of the small fishing boats, or take longer journeys down the coast in his birlinn, now that some of his crew had settled here in Sinclair lands.

She knew it wasn't the same for him, but it wasn't *bad*. Just different. Now he had a greater level of responsibility and even more respect. His days might sometimes be filled with mediating petty squabbles, but hers were as well, and the best part of the day was the hours they spent wrapped in one another's arms, talking about their tasks and planning for their future.

The time would come, not too far in the future, when Da would step down, leaving the Sinclairs in Citrine and Rory's hands.

After all, she was the bravest and most clever of the Sinclair warriors, was she not?

The reminder put a smile on her face, and her hand rose to the brooch pinned to the plaid which covered her heart. Her father, husband, and sisters all agreed that she should have the honor of wearing the Sinclair jewels as a symbol of her skill and responsibility. And every single time she pinned it on, she felt a burst of loyalty, of connection to the past.

Mayhap there *was* something a bit magical to the thing. This *was* the Highlands, after all.

Jaimie interrupted her musing when he took his nephew's hand. "Have ye met Willie, Callan? He's Merrick's oldest son, visiting from his fostering. I met him yesterday, a fine young man."

Callan nodded eagerly as his uncle pulled him away, stopping to wave to their little group. Their departure reminded Citrine of the celebration, and Agata's happy news.

"I'm so pleased for ye, sister," she murmured, her arm still around Rory. "Ye four will be verra happy."

"Well, 'tis still a way off. Possibly after Hogmany, even," Agata said with a pleased smile.

"Have ye told Da and the others?"

Her older sister shook her head. "No' yet. I didnae want to interrupt this celebration with my news." Before Citrine could tell her the news *was* cause for celebration, Agata hurried on. "Speaking of which, look who's *finally* coming over. Jaimie will be so jealous!"

Pearl was bustling toward them, and as she reached them, Agata took baby Mala from her arms with a coo.

"Come to Aunt Agata, my wee Jewel. Are ye no' the most beautiful bairn ever?"

Pearl's laugh sounded a little weak, and Citrine wondered if the new mother was overdoing things. Mala was only a few months old, but Pearl had been running about planning this celebration, in addition to her regular duties. Still, their youngest sister seemed happy.

"*I* ken she's the most beautiful bairn ever, but I ken that about all my nieces and nephews, too. Has anyone seen Saffy and wee Gavin yet?"

Citrine glanced at her husband, but he shook his head.

"No' since they arrived with that lot earlier today," Rory said with a nod. "I cannae imagine how they manage to keep their brood in control…they all seem like little devils!"

Agata laughed, tweaking the babe's nose to elicit a gurgle. "'Tis because their father is the very devil himself, aye, Pearl?" She winked.

Pearl rolled her eyes and planted her fists on her hips. "I've apologized for getting out of that marriage contract a half dozen times since Saffy married the man! How was I supposed to ken all the horrible things they said about him were no' true?"

"Aye, and if ye *had* married the Sutherland Devil," Citrine pointed out, "then ye wouldnae have the fine husband ye *do* have."

"Exactly," Pearl said with a proud nod.

"Where *is* Gregor, anyhow?" Agata asked.

Rory shifted his weight as if not sure how much to say. "He's with Duncan, as usual. Duncan had an…errand."

Pearl and Citrine exchanged an excited glance, knowing what that meant. Over the last year, Citrine had taken her younger sister to see their mother a few times. The visits were always difficult, slightly awkward. The hermit who lived in the grotto, awaiting death as her body slowly failed, was not the mother they remembered. She was a woman obsessed with the past, with stories, and with reading. Visiting her was often a case of sitting quietly while she regaled them with tales from Sinclair history.

Agata and Saffy had not yet met the woman, although they knew of her existence. Citrine had told them both last year, during her autumn visits, and both had gone through disbelief, joy, and confusion as she'd explained. Soon, they'd get to meet Mala Sinclair themselves, and judge for themselves if their mother had returned from the dead, or if she was a stranger to them.

Soon, and mayhap *sooner*, if Gregor and Duncan's errand was successful.

"There they are!" Pearl's breath burst out of her with a relieved sigh, and Citrine's gaze flew to the outer doors. But her younger sister was waving toward the stairs, where Merrick was holding out his hand to help Saffy step down. "Saffy!" she called, waving harder.

Citrine's twin might've only recently given birth, but she fairly flew across the hall to embrace Agata and Pearl. She hugged Citrine as well, but as the twins had spent the better half of the day ensconced in their old room, giggling like girls once again, their embrace was faster.

"Oh, I'm *so* glad to see ye all. Can ye believe we're all together once more?"

Agata smiled and moved a yawning Mala to her other shoulder. "I was saying that to Citrine here. It seems like it took forever!"

"I ken we'll visit one another, but let us make this a tradition." Pearl's pale eyes sparkled with excitement. "Each year at midsummer, we should gather here to celebrate."

"Celebrate what?" Rory asked with a wry grin.

Citrine elbowed him. "*Everything.*"

They were all chuckling when Merrick finally joined them, a scowl on his lips and a baby in his arms.

Pearl was already reaching for her nephew, wee Gavin, the other reason they'd gathered this summer. "Come here, ye wee strong warrior. I heard ye gave yer mother quite the time in the birthing chamber."

Saffy rolled her eyes. "Aye, he was as stubborn as his namesake. 'Tis why we're late. The dear refused to suckle."

"I cannae imagine that," Rory murmured against Citrine's ear, forcing her to lift her fingers to hide her smirk.

Saffy's birth experience had been difficult, and she'd written her twin after Gavin's arrival to tell how scared she'd been. Merrick, who had nine bairns already, had insisted on being present for the birth of this one, his heir.

Apparently, the Sutherland Devil, the most feared man in the Highlands, had almost fainted in the birthing chamber.

"Is that why yer da is frowning so fiercely, eh, ye precious angel?" Pearl cooed at her nephew, smirking as she glanced at Merrick from the corner of her eye.

Merrick, who'd folded his arms across his chest once he'd been relieved of his son, was now scowling across the hall. He didn't answer, but Saffy tucked her hand into his elbow and leaned her cheek against his upper arm.

"Nay, he *always* frowns like this when he gets good news. Aye, husband?"

If anything, Merrick's frown deepened, and he grunted impatiently. Beaming, Saffy turned to her sisters and Rory.

"Merrick's a wee irritated, ye see, because Mary just gave us some delightful news. We're—" She broke off, chuckling, and Merrick rolled his eyes again. Regaining her composure, Saffy tried to nod seriously, but the sparkle in her eyes betrayed her. "We're going to become grandparents!"

When Pearl burst out laughing, Saffy and Citrine joined in. Rory blurted, "*What?*" as Agata's face lit up.

"Mary and Andrew are having a bairn? Oh, how wonderful!"

"'Tisnae wonderful," Merrick growled. "I'm only two-score. Too young to be a grandda. And *ye*," he pointed sternly at his wife, "are *far* too beautiful to be married to a grandda."

Laughing, Saffy captured his hand in hers and brought it to her lips. "I happen to *like* being married to a grandda, assuming it's ye."

With a huff, Merrick pulled her into his embrace. "It just feels *odd*, ye ken?"

"I do, but ye started early, husband." Saffy smiled up at him.

"Willie might be thinking about marriage soon as well. Have ye considered that?"

"Aye," Merrick growled, "but no' for a few years. I made him swear." He sighed. "I suppose I'll have to start thinking about marriage contracts for Adelaide and the other lassies soon."

Citrine chuckled. "I've *met* Maggie. Whoever ye talk into marrying *that* one will have their work cut out for them."

Rory was nodding. "And wee Eva. She's young yet, but if ye're smart, ye willnae let her spend much time with Citrine." When she elbowed him, he dropped a kiss to her forehead. "A family can only take so many firebrands."

Firebrand. He still called her that, although they'd been married for almost a year.

And each time he did, a hint of pride in his voice.

She stretched up on her toes. "I love ye," she whispered in his ear.

The way he squeezed her back, she knew he understood.

"Oh!" Pearl's surprised exclamation had everyone turning to the door.

Gregor had just stepped through, his eyes scanning the crowd until his gaze rested on Pearl. When he gave her a slight nod, she turned and thrust baby Gavin back into his father's arms.

"Excuse me," she said, already hurrying toward her husband.

Then both Agata and Saffy sucked in a breath when they saw who followed their stoic brother-in-law.

Duncan Sinclair, laird of the clan, held the door open for a black-robed figure, bowing solicitously, but careful not to touch her.

Citrine and Rory exchanged a glance.

Mother.

"Is that…?" Agata's whispered question trailed off as Da led the hooded and robed stranger to a chair along the wall, ignoring the murmurs around them.

The woman sank into the seat, as if exhausted from the effort it had taken to travel to the keep, and Da straightened. From across the room, his eyes met Citrine, and he nodded just slightly.

It had been a struggle to convince Mother to attend today's celebration. She was determined to wall herself up from the outside world, but the promise of a glimpse of her grandchildren had been the incentive she needed.

How gut-wrenching it must be, to refuse to embrace her daughters, or touch their babies. But Citrine knew their mother had done it for their own safety, the way she'd left them years ago to die alone.

But mayhap, *now*, she wouldnae be.

Citrine cleared her throat. "Aye," she managed in a hoarse whisper.

In a daze, Saffy reached out and fumbled for Citrine's hand, finally clasping it in a tight grip. "I'm nervous," she admitted.

Agata took a deep breath, still patting wee Mala's bottom. "I'm ready. Do ye think she might want to meet the wee jewel named for her?"

"No' yet." Citrine reached for the sleeping baby, still a little awkward with holding an infant. "For now, let us meet her together."

Saffy and Agata nodded, already moving toward their parents. Rory snagged Citrine's hand.

When she turned to him in confusion, he took the baby from her arms, settling her against his shoulder in a mirror of Merrick's pose. Mayhap he had experience with his niece Charlotte.

Using his hold on her hand, he tugged her closer and dropped his forehead to hers.

"One glows gold in the fire's light," he murmured.

The words never failed to make her smile. It was their way of reminding one another of everything they'd overcome, and that they were stronger together.

"Jewels in the hearthstone's view," she whispered in return.

"Ye are my jewel, Citrine. Never forget that."

She smiled, already feeling stronger. "And ye are my hearthstone. Wherever ye are, 'tis home for me."

"Thank ye for giving me a home, wife. A place to belong. Here in Sinclair lands, and…"

She pressed a kiss to his lips. "And in my heart?"

"Aye," came his rough whisper. "Now go, my love."

Taking a deep breath, Citrine straightened and nodded to her husband. Then she turned and hurried across the hall.

She stepped up beside Saffy, who was still clutching Agata's hand tightly. Pearl moved to her other side, and soon all four of them were holding each other.

Citrine glanced one way, then the other. "Are ye ready?" she whispered.

Saffy's nod was hesitant, Agata's certain, and Pearl was smiling. "Aye," she breathed.

"Well, then." Citrine took a deep breath and straightened her shoulders. Tugging her sisters' hands, she offered them a smile of her own. "Let me introduce ye to yer mother."

And stepping forward, the four Sinclair Jewels met their future.

AUTHOR'S NOTE
On Historical Accuracy

First of all, thank you so much for reading to the end of The Sinclair Jewels series! I hope you love this family as much as I do!

In earlier *Notes*, I've mentioned the inaccuracy of my heroes wearing kilts (*tough patootie*, they're hot!) and the consistent clan mottos/war cries/crests. The crest Saffy and Merrick found at the end of *The Sutherland Devil* belongs to the MacLeods of Lewes, which is how the sisters know they need to go there to find another stone (in this case, the pearl).

However, the MacLeods of Lewes were still a brand-new clan when this story takes place, and you'll just have to forgive the inaccuracies.

The MacLeods are said to have descended from Leod, son of Olaf the Black, who was King of the Isles. In fact, when this story takes place, the Western Isles (including Lewis and Harris, which are technically one island) had just recently joined Scotland. For generations they were ruled by their own king and the Kingdom of the Isles was very powerful.

Leod's two sons became the progenitors of the two branches of the families; Tormod founded the MacLeods of Dunvegan and Harris (made famous in fairy flag folklore) and Torquil founded the MacLeods of Lewes/Lewis.

I've been purposefully vague on *who* exactly Rory's father is, but let's assume, since it's so early in the MacLeods of Lewes' history, that he's a close relative of Leod himself! His oldest brother Tormund is named for their uncle (or great-uncle?), and you'll definitely be meeting him again (see below).

A quick note on Rory's name: You've likely seen the name Ruaidhrí/Ruairi before, often spelled as "Rory". Clan Ruaidhrí was powerful in the Western Isles, and closely connected with the MacLeods. I wanted to acknowledge that briefly by giving my hero the name of a neighboring clan… You know, when he's *not* busy being called the Black Banner!

Next up: leprosy. This disease is bacteria-borne and has been around for millennia. Seriously. It's actually very hard to spread, but the bacteria *does* spread by touch, specifically bodily fluids like mucus. The vast majority of people who come in contact with the bacteria never develop the disease, but it's hard to deny the medieval mindset of contact=contagion.

Mala Sinclair's self-imposed exile is harsh, and likely unnecessary, but effective. Even during the Medieval period, not everyone considered isolation the best solution for those afflicted by leprosy…but "Leper Houses" were run by the Church for just that reason.

After so many years of virtual isolation, it's hard to imagine Mala's mind hasn't been affected, and I tried to convey that. I'm not sure how—if at all—her relationship with her daughters will grow. You'll have to use your own imaginations about that!

Finally, I *know* you're curious about all the bairns mentioned in this series. Do you want to see more of them? You're in luck! Remember wee Charlotte, who was recreating the Battle of Largs (1263; an inconclusive battle in the failed Norwegian attempt to re-take Scotland) with her uncle's wooden ships?

Well, Charlotte and her brother Tav appear in *The Bruce's Angel.* If you're dying to know if Tavish grows up to accomplish his dream and take over as the Black Banner...well, you'll have to read to find out! But I guarantee you've never read a heroine quite like Charlotte MacLeod; she does, indeed, grow up to be someone great (even greater than a pirate!) who makes her clan proud!

Keep reading for a sneak peek of her book, which is the start of a brilliant new, edge-of-your-seat kind of series: Charlie's Angels set in the court of Robert the Bruce!

Finally, I welcome any and all feedback. Did you enjoy this series? Do you want to chat about other historical Scottish romances you've read? You can get in touch with me on Facebook, Bookbub, or my website: www.CarolineLeeRomance.com

If you *are* on Facebook, I welcome you to join my reading group: Caroline's Cohort! We're loads of fun, and I can promise you exclusive sneak peeks at upcoming stories. You'll even get to help me name some characters!

Oh, and don't forget to sign up for my newsletter!

From *The Bruce's Angel*

The last time they'd made love had been on the deck of a pirate's ship.

Of course, at the time, Liam hadn't believed Charlotte when she'd told him of the birlinn's history, but that was probably because she had been giggling as she'd pulled him along the quay that evening toward the innocuous-looking boat. All she'd told him was she wanted to feel the motion of the waves under her, while he moved *over* her, and, well…

How in the hell was a man supposed to deny *that*?

"A pirate boat?" He hummed good-naturedly. "Ye expect me to believe the mighty MacLeod family, the pride of Lewes, harbors *pirates*?"

In the darkness, it was impossible to see the sparkle in her eyes, but he could hear it in her voice as they reached the plank offering access to the birlinn.

"Of course!" she teased. "Ye've never heard of the Black Banner?"

He snorted distractedly, paying more attention to ensuring

she crossed over to the vessel safely. It wasn't necessary; Charlotte MacLeod was many things—talented, passionate, capable —but clumsy wasn't one of them. She trotted across the plank and landed firm-footed on the deck, as if she'd done it many times.

Maybe she had. Her brother Tavish, who was also Liam's friend, was a sailor. Was this his ship?

"Is this Tav's boat?"

She giggled, even as she tugged him toward the stern. "I told ye, my heart...this is the Black Banner's birlinn."

Ah yes, the Black Banner: the child's horror tale, and the likely mythical pirate who stalked the merchants of the Western Isles. And Charlotte expected him to believe he resided here on Lewes.

Liam had arrived in the isles a month ago to formally court the Lady Charlotte, and was still just as delighted with her as he remembered being when they'd met in the Highlands. She wasn't at all proper and ladylike, but met him nose-to-nose.

She'd make a good wife—a good *partner*—and Liam looked forward to formalizing their betrothal with her father, the MacLeod laird.

Until then, he saw no reason not to continue learning all about the woman he'd spend his life with.

They reached the stern platform where the captain would stand, and the helmsmen could lean on the grand rudder.

"Well, my angel..." He pulled her into his arms, lowering his voice to a murmur. "Ye've supposedly dragged me out to the *Black Banner's* boat. Now what?"

She twisted about, managing not to step out of his hold, as she flourished a bundle, which she then shook out to reveal a blanket.

"*Now*, Liam..." She pressed up on her toes, until her lips were beside his ear. "Now you're going to make love to me."

It was her playful tease, more than her words, which set

him hardening under his kilt, but the way she brushed against him as she squirmed out of his arms didn't hurt either.

Before he had time to catch his breath, or do anything more than groan in anticipation, she'd spread the blanket out on the deck, and was tugging at the ties of her gown.

His blood was pounding in anticipation, the way she always made him feel when she matched his passions head on this way, but he had the forethought to glance toward the shore.

This late at night, surely her pale skin and fiery halo of hair would stand out like a torch?

She guessed what concerned him. "That's what makes it *fun*, Liam," she whispered in that husky voice of hers, and he gave up caring about propriety.

If she, the willful and beautiful daughter of the laird, was willing to buck convention for *him*, who was he to argue?

"Aye, my angel." With a smile, Liam made short work of his own clothing, adding them to the pile on the deck beside the blanket. Truthfully, he was glad his kilt wasn't too complicated, because when she began to peel away her chemise, his fingers—and his mind—turned into lumps of rock.

His Charlotte had always preferred making love out-of-doors, but usually they made do without fully disrobing. It hadn't been often he'd been able to drink in the sight of her this way, standing nude and proud, managing to look strong and capable, even on the deck of a sailing ship.

Liam drank in the sight of her, grateful beyond measure to have found such an incredible woman.

I love you.

He needed her to know that, but he couldn't seem to make his voice work.

Then she was reaching for him, pulling him down beside her so they could cradle one another with their arms, and he had more important things on his mind.

"Ye're sure about this?" he murmured against her skin, as he trailed kisses from her neck to her breast. "Sure 'tis safe?

She arched against him with a moan. "Can ye no' feel the power of the surf under us, my heart?"

He was too busy to focus on her poetry, but knew she was right. The boat rocked in time with the waves, the way he wanted to rock atop her.

"I need ye, Liam," she panted. "I want ye to be mine."

"Yer only."

"My only," she agreed, breathless.

His mouth was occupied for the next little while, and the sound of her small cries and mews was enough to keep him standing stiffly at attention. He stroked her softly, marveling at her enthusiasm.

God Almighty, but she was ready for him.

When she curved against him once more, he knew she was as ready as he was. Grasping her thighs, he slid her closer, settling himself between her legs as she writhed on the thin blanket.

"Liam!" she cried, part plea, part command. "Donae stop, please."

"Aye," he breathed, his hand tracing up her chest to rest against her cheek. "Ye're so hot, so passionate, Charlotte. I'm afraid ye and I will both burn up, leaving nothing but cinders." It was a joke between them, when he called her *Char*.

"If we do," she panted beneath him, "'twill be your fault as much as mine. Now stop delaying!"

"As my lady commands."

When he finally pressed home, she cried out in pleasure.

Or mayhap it was joy.

She met him, thrust for thrust, as the familiar pressure built behind Liam's bollocks.

He'd been with other women, aye, but this was *Charlotte*,

and making love to Charlotte was like nothing he'd ever experienced before.

He watched her face as she contorted, and marveled at how well he could read her, despite the near-darkness. Even without her wrapped around him, he could tell when she was close. The pleasure mixed with frustration he saw when she met his gaze told her everything he needed to know.

He dropped a hand between their joined bodies and stroked the pearl nestled within her curls.

She gasped his name, and he felt her muscles contracting around him.

It took everything in him not to roar her name, not to beg for God's mercy, the way she was doing, but as he spilled his seed deep inside her, his only indication was the way he stiffened against her.

Still, they both collapsed with groans, breathing heavily. Under him, she went limp, her arms and legs dropping their holds on his body to pool, boneless, against the coverlet. And she was grinning.

Reverently, Liam leaned down to place a kiss at the corner of her lips. Then another against her neck.

"I love ye," he whispered. When she didn't respond, he hoisted himself up on his elbows to meet her eyes. "I love ye, Char. I love everything about ye. Yer mind, yer passion. I'll love ye until my dying breath."

She cupped his cheek, her lips drawn into a smile glorious to behold. "Of course ye will. For I love ye, and nae one will say otherwise."

And he knew, beyond a shadow of a doubt, he'd found his forever.

***

Charlotte would never forget the day her life changed forever.

She was holding Liam's hand as they strolled through the courtyard, and a messenger arrived with a scroll. Her love had read it, then looked at her with pain in his lovely blue eyes. She took it from his limp fingers and read King Robert Bruce's summons.

Liam was an important man to their King. He'd fought beside the Bruce at Linlithgow and Dumbarton, and had been one of the first Scot warriors into Perth when the Bruce took back the royal burgh. King Robert trusted Liam, and she was proud of him.

Proud someone as brave and trustworthy as he had chosen to fall in love with her.

It was perfectly reasonable he'd be called back to his duties, and she loved him for it. Still, as she'd looked into his eyes, she couldn't help feeling…scared.

There was something in his expression, which seemed to be warning her, the simple future they'd planned might not come to be.

Saying goodbye to him was one of the hardest things she'd ever done, and as she stood outside the gates and watched him ride toward the shore, and the boat which would take him to his royal cousin, Charlotte reminded herself of their love.

Liam *loved* her and would return to her.

But never once did he look back.

A month passed, and no matter how certain she still was of her feelings for him, that little fact continued to eat at her.

She retreated to her room and curled up on her bed—the bed in which Liam had once held her in his arms and whispered such sweet words after one of the rare occasions they'd made love indoors—and let the tears fall.

She spent the afternoon there, which is why she hadn't heard news of the visitor. It wasn't until her father sent for her that Charlotte realized she needed to make herself presentable.

My life isnae *falling apart. Liam loves me, and I love him. We* will *be together.*

So why did her sense of dread only increase as she approached her father's solar?

Da was waiting inside, holding a piece of parchment and paying her no attention, as usual. The same couldn't be said of his companion.

"Lady Charlotte," the man welcomed her, his eyes on her breasts under the rumpled gown. "When ye are my wife, ye will learn to comport yerself, I trust?"

Her hands curled into fists in the wool of her skirts. "What?" she asked hoarsely.

The man—wasn't he one of the MacDonald's younger sons?—waved one hand dismissively. "Ye look as if ye've *slept* in that thing, woman. And yer eyes are all puffy. Nae wife of mine will appear less than perfect." He lifted a shoulder and turned toward her father. "I'm looking for a biddable ornament with admirable assets, MacLeod."

"Ye'll get Charlotte, and ye'll be grateful," Da growled, still examining the document.

Charlotte was having trouble breathing, and her pulse had become a dull roar in her ears. "Da?" she managed to choke out. "What…?"

What was going on?

Wife of his?

Was that a marriage contract her father was reading?

Marriage to a MacDonald?

But Liam...

Liam was the man she loved. The one who'd vowed to spend forever with her.

Her father finally looked up and met her eyes. "The MacDonald and I have decided yer future, girl." He gestured to the other man. "John MacDonald is willing to marry ye."

Charlotte's mouth dropped open.

Willing?

Was this another attempt to forge an alliance with a clan, who was their enemy more often as not?

Ignoring John—and the way he was staring at her chest and licking his lips—Charlotte stepped toward her father, knowing she had to convince him. "Da, Liam and I…we are in love." She heard the note of desperation in her voice, but couldn't silence it. "We have an agreement."

To his credit, her father *did* shift his weight awkwardly, as if affected by her words. But then he shook his head and slammed the contract down on the desk in front of him.

"Ye would put yer own wants ahead of yer clan's future?" he growled, reaching for the stylus. "John is an ambitious man and will do us all proud."

"I donae *want* an ambitious husband, Da!" She was torn between tears and anger, her nails pressing into her palms to hold back the urge to scream or hit something. "I want Liam! He's kinsman to the King," she added in desperation, taking another step toward her father, her hand out in supplication. "Surely that makes him a good ally?"

Da had pressed his lips together then, his palm flat against the desk, as he'd leaned forward and seemed to consider her words. Charlotte held her breath and tried to stave off the horror with hope.

Even John quit his study of her *assets* and focused on her father. Her blood was pounding in her ears, and she found herself praying.

But when he finally shook his head, she felt her knees go weak with defeat.

"Liam Bruce cannae marry ye, lass, because he's betrothed to another."

That's when her knees gave out on her completely, and Charlotte sank to the floor. Her palms flattened against the cool flagstones, as if she could draw some of their strength into her shaking bones.

Betrothed? *Her* Liam? The man who'd sworn to love her until his dying breath...was engaged to another?

"Betrothed?" she asked weakly, tears threatening.

Da nodded brusquely, seeming uncomfortable with her display of emotion. "He's a Bruce, lass. Of course his royal cousin would see to his betrothal, some Lowland heiress with a powerful father."

Oh God.

Two fat tears trailed down her cheeks and plopped onto the back of her hands, as she stared down at what felt like her only anchor to the world.

Had her heart stopped beating altogether?

Betrothed to another.

I'll love ye until my dying breath.

Oh God.

Her father cleared his throat. "An alliance with the MacDonalds is what's best for me, and ye'll do as ye're told, girl."

John spoke up again then, his voice smug and oily. "I want a wife who understands her place."

A wife's place was beside her husband, was it not?

In confusion, still not entirely sure she understood what was happening, Charlotte lifted her gaze from the floor to stare at the stranger she was supposed to marry.

"Her *place*, John?" she whispered, allowing her anger to seep into her voice.

He didn't notice, judging by his smirk as he crouched beside her. "Behind me. Or *under* me, as the case may be." He reached out and grabbed her chin, forcing her to meet his eyes. "I want heirs, ye ken."

Before she could spit her defiance, he thrust her away from him and stood in one motion, turning toward her father once more. "Let us sign the betrothal, MacLeod, so I can escort yer daughter to her new home and start instructing her in her new duties."

Da grunted as he scrawled something across the bottom of the parchment and held the stylus out for the younger man to do the same.

Hollowly, Charlotte watched as her father reach for the wax to press his seal into the document, and knew her life would never be the same.

And she was right.

———

Okay, look. Charlotte and Liam's story involves treason, espionage, piracy on the high seas, the Queen of Scotland, and A Perfect Kiss. Sound exciting? Grab *The Bruce's Angel*, free for a limited time, and get ready for an incredible new adventure series!

ABOUT THE AUTHOR

USA Today bestselling author Caroline Lee has been reading romance for so long that her fourth-grade teacher used to make her cover her books with paper jackets, but it wasn't until she (mostly) grew up that she realized she could WRITE it too. So she did.

Caroline is living her own little Happily Ever After in NC with her husband, sons, daughter Princess Wiggles. She thinks it's important to note that she made it all the way through grad school (her second history degree) without knowing how to touch-type (she taught herself to type only a few years ago and APPARENTLY lesrned imcorrectly--*learned incorrectly*, a fact which she's only now realizing, as other authors point and laugh). Caroline adores rodents, goes through laptops like Pez, and never met a whisk(e)y she didn't like. She's also pretty funny in person. Promise.

You can find her at www.CarolineLeeRomance.com.

OTHER BOOKS BY CAROLINE LEE

Want the scoop on new books? Join Caroline's Cohort, an exclusive reader group! Or sign up for my mailing list by texting "Caroline" to 42828 to get started!

Hilarious Scottish RomComs:
The Hots for Scots (8 books)
Highlander Ever After (3 books)
Bad in Plaid (6 books)
Second-Chance Manor (2 books)
Those Kilted Bastards (4 books)
Surprise! Dukes (5 books)

Steamy Scottish Historicals:
The Sinclair Jewels (4 books)
The Highland Angels (5 books)

Sensual Historical Westerns:
Black Aces (3 books)
Sunset Valley (3 books)
Everland Ever After (10 books)

The Sweet Cheyenne Quartet (6 books)

Sweet Contemporary Westerns
Quinn Valley Ranch (5 books)
River's End Ranch (14 books)
The Cowboys of Cauldron Valley (7 books)
The Calendar Girls' Ranch (6 books)

Click **here** to find a complete list of Caroline's books.

*Sign up for Caroline's Newsletter to receive exclusive content and freebies, as well as first dibs on her books! Or if newsletters aren't your thing, follow her on **Bookbub** for a quick, concise new release alert every time she publishes a book!*

www.ingramcontent.com/pod-product-compliance
Lightning Source LLC
Chambersburg PA
CBHW061249120726
48001CB00001B/221